A Conflict of Interest
Anna Adams

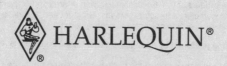

HARLEQUIN®

TORONTO • NEW YORK • LONDON
AMSTERDAM • PARIS • SYDNEY • HAMBURG
STOCKHOLM • ATHENS • TOKYO • MILAN • MADRID
PRAGUE • WARSAW • BUDAPEST • AUCKLAND

Recycling programs
for this product may
not exist in your area.

ISBN-13: 978-0-373-78343-4

A CONFLICT OF INTEREST

Printed in U.S.A.

ABOUT THE AUTHOR

Anna Adams wrote her first romance on the beach in wet sand with a stick. These days she uses modern tools to write the kind of stories she loves best—romance that involves everyone in the family, and often the whole community. Love between two people, like the proverbial stone in a lake—the ripples of their feelings spread and contract, bringing conflict and "help" from the people who care most about them.

Anna is in the middle of one of those stories, with her own hero. From Iceland to Hawaii and points in between they've shared their lives with children and family and friends who've become family. Right now they're living in a small Southern town, whose square has become the model for the one where much of the action happens in Honesty, Virginia. In fact, Anna wrote much of *A Conflict of Interest* in a coffee shop looking out at the courthouse that features in the story. All this living and loving gives Anna plenty of fodder to dream up stories of real love set in real life. Come along and live them with her!

Books by Anna Adams

HARLEQUIN SUPERROMANCE

To Missy, because the roads are empty without you.

And to June, Alan, Adam and Brandon,
good friends who've become family.

CHAPTER ONE

BITS OF ICE PLINKED against the courtroom windows, to the odd accompaniment of whispering fans that dispersed the heat of too many bodies packed into one small space. The defense attorney, a walking cliché of paunch and righteous anger, set a composition book in front of Dr. Maria Keaton on the witness stand.

"Do you recognize this diary?" Buck Collier pointed with his thick finger.

Maria stared at the marbleized cover, rubbed almost gray. Her patient, Griff Butler, had scrawled shapes into the cardboard, bearing down so hard he'd drilled red and blue ink beneath the surface. He'd written words and then crossed them out with heavy marker. He'd drawn muscle-bound men firing guns that sprayed bullets across the mottled cover.

And he'd tried to make her read the pages, swollen with his secrets.

He'd had a crush. Sometimes patients got them, but as they healed, they also found out they didn't truly love their therapists.

But one look at the man behind the judge's bench, just above her, made her reconsider. The man whose gaze she'd avoided because his black eyes made her painfully aware that inappropriate, nearly mind-drugging attraction could also afflict her. Judge Jake Sloane didn't even have to move to capture her attention.

Soon after she'd moved to Honesty, he'd said hello at a party and taken her hand just as someone else called to him from across the buffet table. She'd let go, but the low timbre of his voice had touched her. She'd dragged her hand out of midair to hold it close to her stomach. With a nod, Jake had strode away, his lean body cutting a swath through the crowd.

Attraction that felt more like instant addiction made her wary. After that, she'd hung back, watching Jake at town meetings and the food bank where they both volunteered. She'd waited for her ridiculous crush to wane.

Since the moment she'd answered the bailiff's summons to the courtroom, she'd been uncomfortably aware of Jake, leaning back in his chair, his sharp features focused, totally belying his body's false image of indifference.

"Dr. Keaton?" Buck's imperious tone cut through Maria's thoughts. "The journal. What's in it?"

"I don't know." She forced her attention back to the defense attorney's sweating face.

Buck waited, letting her reply echo in the room. "You may be ashamed to answer my questions, but the court demands you tell us what's in that book." The man's beady blue eyes glittered with anticipation.

"I didn't read the journal. Your client insisted he killed his parents. I had to call the police. That's everything I know."

He stared at her, his skepticism a big show for the jury. "You're trying to make us believe you never opened that book?"

"Griff never let it out of his reach."

Buck Collier continued to watch her, but again he didn't speak. She'd used that same method too many times to be felled by it, and matched his silence with her own. He cracked first.

"You never asked to read it? He never asked you to?"

"He did." He'd tried to make her, pulling it out of his book bag, hauling it out of the back of his pants, letting it slip from his folded jacket. He'd shoved it to her floor the day she'd finally called the police. "I couldn't."

"You couldn't? You were too involved with him to read aloud his intimate feelings?" Collier waved his hand as bitterness crept, acidlike, into the pit of Maria's stomach. The attorney performed a slow, surprisingly graceful twirl toward the jury box. "Didn't you tell him to write those entries?"

"I suggested that writing about his feelings might clarify them. Writing about them with me in mind as a potential reader would have made the *exercise* pointless," she said, her tone emphasizing that the journal had been a kind of prescription.

Collier gave her a smile that felt like a pat on the head for a troublesome child. A wordless *That's the best you can do?*

It damn well was, because it was the truth.

Buck glided closer, a magician setting up his best trick. "You know what that book contains?"

"I do now." Movement at her side drew her glance. Jake Sloane, deceptively relaxed, stared at her, and her throat tried to swell shut. She gave herself a mental shake.

She'd called the police because Griff had insisted he'd shot his parents. To this day, she doubted he'd actually done the crime. Regardless of whether he'd confessed to get her attention or truly had killed his mother and father, he needed help, and she had to get Jake out of her head and concentrate on her former patient.

"Dr. Keaton, why won't you answer me?"

Behind Collier, Gil Daley, the prosecutor, leaned around his opponent's body and shot her a warning glance.

"It's your client's journal, Mr. Collier." Sitting back, Maria folded her hands in her lap, careful to erase all signs of tension. "I never opened it."

"Uh-huh." He took it back, weighing it in his hand, his glance filled with disdain. "Review it for us. A stirring tale of young love on the psychologist's couch?"

Subtle as an anvil to the skull. Tittering rustled among the citizens of Honesty, Virginia, who'd arrived at court in time for tickets to this circus. Maybe they didn't need proof.

Maria stifled a compulsion to face Jake and declare her innocence. Instead, she stared at the boy with the cold, blank eyes. Buck had dressed him in a nice black suit of mourning, but no one could show Griff how to pretend he felt—anything.

"I've never touched it. I haven't opened the cover."

"What did you touch, Dr. Keaton?"

On the raised bench, the judge moved in his squeaking leather chair.

Daley sprang from his seat. "Your Honor, I—"

Buck waved a dismissing hand at Gil. "Question withdrawn. I'm sorry, folks, but I get hot under the collar when justice is perverted." Buck shook the book at Maria. "You know how Griff used this."

The prosecutor spoke out for the eighth time during Maria's cross-examination. "The defense asks the impossible. How does he expect the witness to testify to the contents of a journal she's never read?"

Buck turned on Gil.

Scowling, Daley sat.

"If the prosecutor would maintain his seat and the peace, we could drill to the truth." Like a powerful figure on a Michelangelo ceiling, Buck pointed at Maria. "This woman made my client write the diary. Not only has she read it, they've read it together. With every entry, they relived their sexual encounters. She thought up new—"

Maria froze. The packed courtroom erupted in whispers of "I told you so," and shrill "No's," all backed by a slithering undercurrent of gasps, which Jake cut off with a curt, "Order."

Maria heard and saw it all through a revolted haze.

The prosecutor leaped to his feet. "I object—"

Jake lifted his hand. "Hold on, Mr. Daley." He hit a key on the laptop in front of him. "Step forward, gentlemen, and not another word out of anyone, or I'll clear the gallery."

As he sat forward, he glanced at Maria, searching for the truth. Every false indication of indolence fled as he raked her with his eyes. Shame—unexpected, unwelcome and totally unwarranted—made her skin sizzle.

Determined to face him down, she willed Gil aside when he stepped between her and Jake to have his say in furious whispers. Buck drawled a response, but he grabbed the ledge of Jake's desk with his fists and betrayed the hard-fighting lawyer behind his mellow, country-boy mask.

Jake covered the microphone. Control vibrated in his husky tone, though Maria couldn't discern most of his words. When she heard him say her name, she became even more uneasy, but Gil still blocked her view.

Jake's low voice emphasized his warning to the attorneys with the words "personal attack" and "contempt." He finished with a louder "Stand back."

A red flush slowly spread from Collier's collar. Gil turned away, saying respectfully, "Thank you, Your Honor."

Collier retook the podium at the end of his table. "What's in the notebook, Ms. Keaton?"

"Doctor," Gil said.

Jake swung calm but killing eyes toward the prosecutor, who sat. Jake prompted Buck with raised brows. All the while, Maria either sensed or imagined the judge's focus on her. And she could barely breathe.

"Dr. Keaton?" Distaste dripped from Buck's tone.

Maria refused to act the defensive, sex-crazed, older woman part he'd dreamed up. "Griff offered me the notebook." Now that the accusation was out in the open, she kept her voice calm and rational. The law required her to report a crime, but she didn't have to throw away her client or her own reputation. "I never read it."

Buck laughed as if she'd told a joke that wasn't in the least funny. "You've seen these pages how many times?"

"Asked and answered," Gil said. "Ad nause—"

"Gentlemen," Jake said, as if nothing about this situation troubled him in the least, "I've warned you."

Buck's complacent expression faltered. "You can't deny Griff wanted you to see what he'd written."

She'd come to this courtroom with one goal in

mind, to make the jury see the kid needed help, not a prison sentence. Instead, she was defending herself against Collier's plan to make her seem like a pervert on the prowl in her own practice.

"You opened Griff up to his feelings, didn't you, Dr. Keaton?"

Revolting filth of a man.

The courtroom spectators whispered. Jake's chair squeaked, like nails raking a chalkboard, and she felt him looking at her. She refused to meet his gaze. She'd put distance between herself and Jake after she'd begun to treat his daughter, Leila. The last thing Leila Sloane or any of Maria's clients needed was for their therapist to be suspected of seducing an under-aged teen.

"My clients don't walk out of textbooks. Textbook answers won't always help them."

Gil leaned forward, warning her again.

"I hear you took a suicidal teen mountain climbing," Collier said.

"We climbed the side of a ridge at a camp." And she'd been scared half out of her wits.

"You also ran a marathon?"

"A half one." With a woman who couldn't stand still for fear her father's sexual abuse would catch up with her.

For another client too afraid of public speaking to make a simple speech in his own boardroom, Maria had listened to late-night rehearsals on the phone until her ear was as cauliflowerlike as the most inept boxer's.

She'd cooked meals and walked labyrinths and finally gone to the police when Griff Butler had refused to retract the confession she still doubted.

"You know how to make people comfortable. You make them trust you."

She eyed him but said nothing.

"And you used what Griff Butler said in this notebook to make him your—"

She planted both business-casual heels on the floor. This man would not make her look incapable, even to save a kid she cared for. "I don't know what he wrote."

"Open it," Buck said. "Read the pages you shared with my client at each meeting—including the ones outside your office."

"I've never met Griff outside my office, Mr. Collier."

"You're formal with me, *Dr.* Keaton." He made her title an insult. "But you dropped the decorum with *Griffy,* didn't you?"

She let herself smile. The prototypical Southern lawyer had made an error. "Griff claims I called him that?" Insecurity plagued the boy. He'd feared that no one, not even his own mother and father, had loved him.

"Open the book, Dr. Keaton."

She stared at Buck, pretending his peremptory tone amused her.

"Objection," Gil said. "The defense is harassing Dr. Keaton. She has sworn under oath several times that she never read these pages. How can they be relevant?"

Jake's exaggerated stillness was a warning. His bland expression suggested he'd expected Gil to come up with something more effective, which troubled Maria. At last, Jake looked at the defense. "Get to the point, Mr. Collier. Skip the commentary."

"Did you have an affair with my underage client, Dr. Keaton?"

It hurt. Against her will, she glanced at Griff, who stared at nothing.

"Answer me, Dr. Keaton. Don't look at that boy."

"I did not have an affair with Griff. I wanted him to be well. I'm his psychologist. Nothing more."

"You *were* his so-called therapist. After you broke doctor-client privilege, I believe his aunt fired you?"

His aunt was the only one left to fire her after

his parents died. "Griff, you know why I told the police what you said."

Jake's seat came upright with a scream of springs. "Dr. Keaton, you will not—"

Buck pointed a vindictive finger. "You can't control this boy now that he's come to his senses. He understands you abused him."

"Your Honor." Gil went off like a rocket.

Maria turned to the jury, Griff's last hope. He needed treatment, and they held the power. But Buck had come up with the perfect offensive defense. If the jury thought she'd seduced a kid in her care, they could set a possibly murderous boy free on their own unsuspecting community, on his younger cousins and their parents.

"I never hurt Griff. He and I discussed only the problems that brought him to my office, and none of those problems included an inappropriate relationship between us. I care about this boy as I care about all my clients, but I did not sleep with him."

Jake banged his gavel once. "Dr. Keaton, Collier, Daley, this remains my courtroom, and you're all perilously close to contempt."

"I'm sorry." She turned to him. His black gaze was a wall that bounced her back. "No one seems to realize what's at stake for that kid."

"You were telling us how deeply you *care* for

my client, Dr. Keaton." Collier leaped on her apparent weakness. "Enough to ruin his future after he rejected your sexual advances?"

Jake turned in his chair, silent, menacing. Behind Maria, the jury rustled like debris swept up in a tornado.

"Stop, Mr. Collier, or I'll walk you to a cell myself." Jake's voice seemed to shatter Collier's bloated confidence. "Bailiff, take the jury out."

The men and women stepped on each other's heels, trying to size up Maria. She glanced at Jake. His thoughts were as plain as Buck's. Griff's defense had already created at least one instance of reasonable doubt.

She turned to stare after the jury. Would her word be enough for them? What would happen to the rest of her clients when word of Griff and Buck's story got out? She was no martyr. What would happen to her and her practice? Her future?

The soft thud of Jake's fist dropping onto his desk made Maria jump, but she couldn't look him in the eye. She didn't want him to think the worst of her.

For two years she'd been trying to make this small town her home, ignoring speculative looks from new neighbors who were reluctant to accept someone they considered unconventional. But she'd had compassion on her side.

Over time, she'd helped enough loved ones to be allowed her place in Honesty, and she'd grabbed it with both hands and all her heart.

And then her heart had drawn her toward Jake Sloane. After the party, she'd remembered only him, exuding power borne of his comfort in his own desirable skin.

They'd met many times. She'd sneaked glances at him as they'd worked together on food lines and discussed changes on the Friends of the Library board. She'd cleaned litter on the edges of town with a group that included him. But before any relationship could develop, he'd become off-limits.

One morning, his daughter Leila had made an appointment with Maria. During her sessions Leila had revealed arms and thighs scarred from the cutting she'd started after her parents' acrimonious divorce.

Leila didn't want her father to know she needed help. According to her, he thrived in his own detached world, and he didn't care to be disturbed. She swore her father was so neutral he'd try to argue both sides of sin at the pearly gates. A bad quality in a father, but it guaranteed he'd run an objective courtroom.

Maria might have kept her distance from her patient's father like a good little psychologist, but she sure as hell didn't want Jake Sloane, the man she'd wanted from across many rooms, to think she'd seduce a kid who depended on her.

"Buck," the judge said, "I don't want any more of your opinions. If you have a theory with merit, share that, but no more innuendo."

"Your Honor, I'm allowed—"

Jake held up his hand. "To argue an alternative theory, which you are not doing. You're not suggesting Dr. Keaton murdered the Butlers?"

"No, sir," Buck spluttered.

"You're not allowed to slander a witness. Stop testifying for your client. If he has something to tell the court about Dr. Keaton, the jury wants to hear it from him." Next, he turned to the prosecutor. "Mr. Daley, we'll take a brief recess so you can instruct your witness on protocol, and so she can regain her composure. All of you, remember why you're here, or you'll be giving me your excuses from jail."

Jake rose, impossibly tall, his face as harsh and fine as a sculpture. His long, capable fingers grazed the desk, just inches from Maria.

Her heart beat in her throat.

He stared at her as if she'd grabbed him, as if he could see all the unsettling images in her head, of his hands on her, of her whispering, *I've wanted you so long.*

Maria almost laughed. She was a freaking casebook. Young woman whose father had died when she was too young. She'd searched for authority, even while she'd rejected it.

Falling for Jake was a cliché, and yet she couldn't breathe as he walked away. His robes ballooned, and the scent of clean male brushed her. He left through a door behind the paneled wall, and she fought with sheer will to stay upright.

CHAPTER TWO

GRIFF SCRAPED BACK his chair and followed a deputy out of the courtroom. Buck walked behind his client, glowering at Maria.

Gil headed to the witness box then hustled her to the hall, bending close to her so no one in the gallery could hear his anger. "What are you thinking? I warned you Buck would pull something. You should know how to handle him." With a hand at her elbow, he urged her toward the office he was using during the trial. He shut the door behind them.

"I didn't expect what they said." She could hardly explain that she didn't want Jake to see whether Griff had spun credible fantasies in that diary. "Who would believe I'd—"

"The jury," Gil said. "Buck's hoping they'll believe you ratted Griff out to get back at him for not wanting a relationship with you. You've even got Sloane looking uncertain."

"He's not supposed to choose a side."

"That's how bad you're hurting my case. You've got a guy who never sides with anyone, giving you the once-over because you have an urge to nurture a kid who killed his parents."

"He doesn't belong in prison, Gil. He needs care."

"He needs bars and round-the-clock guards. If a kid his age can kill his parents, what comes next?"

"What if he didn't do it? He tried every way he could think of to make me read that journal. What if his confession is one more trick, but it got out of hand?"

"What if you're the most gullible human being ever born? You'd better stop letting your heart bleed for Griff and think about where you belong."

"I'm no idiot. I know I could lose my job." Even innocence couldn't wash away the stain of suspicion in a small town. "But this kid came to me for help, and I feel responsible."

Gil pulled out a chair at the room's lone table and, after she sat, took the seat across from her. "Are you kidding? You'll have so many calls tomorrow you'll have to find a partner. This town hardly ever gets a good look at a harlot."

"That's hilarious," she said, as if she were

talking through ground glass. "I'm not a harlot, and getting that reputation won't pay my mortgage."

"Then calm down and let's get back to our plan. Collier has you on the run, but use the skills that make you a good therapist. You can see where he's leading you. Don't follow."

She pressed her hands to her cheeks. She had to get Jake out of her head.

Gil sat back, folding his hands between his legs. "I have to ask you the question."

"Did I sleep with Griff?"

"Thanks. I didn't know how to phrase it."

"You don't have to use kid gloves."

"You look rattled."

"He's a kid. I'm twice his age."

"I wish you'd told me how he felt about you."

"It was a kid's crush. Any first-year psych student has heard of transference. I figured he'd get over it." Just as she was supposed to get over this crazy thing for the judge.

"Do you think his parents might have found out about—"

"There was nothing to find out. I shouldn't have to explain that to you. Griff said they argued when his parents canceled his senior trip to Cancun because they found ecstasy in his room. It had nothing to do with me."

Gil walked around the table, scanning her face. "You may never know for sure what caused the violence in that home. Griff's obviously a liar, but we found no drugs when we searched the house."

"He was living with his aunt and uncle for over a month before you executed the search warrant."

"My point is, I can't have him searched daily unless he's in jail. If we don't get him put away, he'll be in constant contact with his little cousins and the kids at school." Gil turned toward the window. "And anyone he passes in the street."

Maria saw exactly how naive she'd been— with the district attorney. "Does everyone get away with lying to me these days?" Talk about losing her touch. "You tricked me into testifying, when you planned to lock him up all along."

"I'm responsible to Channing and Ada Butler, and the family they left behind. You, of all people, should understand the kind of violence that kid's got in him if he shot his parents."

They'd reached an impasse. "I do, but something caused all this."

"Other than just plain evil?" He shrugged. "Don't let Collier throw you and we'll get this kid off the streets. Deny the affair, but stay calm. Don't make Griff look like a victim."

"I know how to handle the truth." She tugged at the neckline of her blouse, trying to cover any curves that made her look like a woman.

He assessed her. "I believe Griff's dying to take you down because you didn't sleep with him, but that version of the story isn't as salacious as a woman wanting revenge against a kid who's dumped her."

"Is Buck going to read that journal out loud?"

"I would if I had it." He shook his head. "I don't know what he'll do. If they read it in the jury room and believe it, we're still sunk."

"I didn't do it."

Not even Gil would look her in the eye. "Answer only Buck's questions. Don't put Griff's future before yours—and don't give the jury an excuse to burn my evidence."

"I am most of your evidence."

"Exactly." He opened the door, but checked to see if anyone else was near. Only the bailiffs, impervious as marble. "Griff can explain away the blood on his shoes and clothes by saying he was checking on his parents. You're the only proof against him that he can't explain without calling you bad names, so I'd prefer you take the high road and not get arrested for contempt."

"At least I won't be alone."

Nor were they now. The women's room door

opened and a tall, tired woman came out, stumbling when she saw Maria.

She took glasses from her pocket and slid them on, the better either to stare with scorn at her nephew's doctor, or to shield her own doubt.

But Angela Hammond couldn't hide her pain, and Maria's instinct was to reach out to her. Angela huffed and made her deliberate way back to the courtroom.

"Don't let that bother you," Gil said.

"Because she won't be the only one turning her back on me?" She tried not to sound as frightened as she felt. This town was her first real home. She wanted to help Griff Butler, but at the cost of everything that made her who she was?

Gil took her arms and spun her around to face him. "I don't like that tone. You're not thinking of backing out?"

At that moment, Jake came out of another door. He stared from Gil's grasping fingers to Maria's face. One dark eyebrow went up, and the cold father Leila had described disappeared.

The silence grew thick and hot, but Maria, adept at feeling another person's pain, could not read Jake.

Did he think she'd been flirting with the prosecutor? Working her apparently irresistible wiles?

Without seeming to move, Jake ended up toe

to toe with Gil. "What the hell do you think you're doing?" His furious question had the power to shake the building on its foundation.

Gil took a step back then looked embarrassed about backing away from another man. "Talking to my client." He stared at Jake. "Your Honor."

"Which led you to put your hands on her?" Jake glanced at Maria. "Are you all right?"

"I'm…" She meant to say *fine,* but she went blank.

No one had ever protected her. She was the product of freewheeling nomads…a mother who'd perfected her skills for any job that came with a chance to attract a man, and a father who'd dropped in once in a while, always promising Maria and her sister, Bryony, they'd be a family. Someday.

Their dad had "borrowed" from their piggy banks, talked their mother out of their minuscule college funds and eventually died in a boating accident with his latest squeeze, bolting across a lake with the money they'd snatched off a poker table in a so-called friendly, floating game.

Maria remembered everything about his last departure, down to the smear of mud on his rounded shoe heel and the stitching on his carry-on bag.

Typical. The mind under stress returns to a

similar episode and handles the new stress the same way. "I'm fine," she said, as she had then, over and over again.

She wrapped her hand around Gil's upper arm to show Jake that the prosecutor wasn't the problem. "We were just going back."

"Daley."

Gil turned weary, slightly petulant eyes on Jake. "Sir, this case is getting to all of us, but you don't have to be suspicious of me."

"I'll agree Buck can be persuasive when he plays good old boy, but I'm not sure you want to intimidate your own witness."

"You're on the verge of saying something inappropriate to a prosecutor and his witness in a case you're hearing."

Jake rounded on Gil again. "I don't give a damn if you're planning to try my grandmother next. Touch a woman in my courthouse and I'll give you plenty of reason to ask for my recusal. Again, I ask, are you all right, Dr. Keaton?"

"Fine." Her tongue seemed mostly stuck to the roof of her mouth. "You misunderstood."

Jake's twisted smile managed to suggest she made a habit of protecting violent men. "Gil isn't dragging you into court?"

She overreacted, as would any woman who cared for a man she hardly knew and didn't want him to think she'd let… "I'm not some sick woman who only hangs around with kids who kill their parents and guys who manhandle women."

"Excuse me, but will you both shut up, and let's get on with this trial?" Gil grabbed at the knot of his tie as if he were fighting its grip. "I beg your pardon, Judge, but I've come too far with this case to risk a mistrial now."

"The prosecutor is right, Dr. Keaton." Jake looked faintly startled at having to be reminded. He crossed in front of them and opened the door to his chambers.

His absence left a vacuum, as if the force of his personality had taken all the good oxygen with him.

"Why did he come this way?" Maria asked.

"I've seen him pace this hall before when we've had troubling cases. You're surprised this one bothers him?"

Trembling threatened to take her legs out from under her. "He thinks I might be the guilty one."

Gil nodded. "But you can fix everything."

"Don't try to play me anymore. I came to you because the law required it, and I thought you might see that Griff was in trouble. You just want me to help you lock him away for life."

He nodded. "Now you're seeing the light. Let's go."

The instant she set foot inside the courtroom, every head turned. A wave of disdain slammed into her.

For a second, she was back in elementary school. One of the Keaton girls, whose mother, Gail, showed up in big hair, brilliant-colored flowing faux silks and excesses of fake gold—when she remembered to attend parent conferences at all. Maria breathed in, preparing to run the gauntlet. She lifted her chin and pretended that nothing could touch her. She'd made peace with her mother and her past. She didn't fight that kind of battle any longer.

She walked to a seat behind Gil's table. Within moments, the jury returned. A door behind the bench opened and Jake came in. His eyes scanned her face, and she felt as if his fingers had followed.

She shuddered.

Her whole body went hot and then cold. She didn't enjoy feeling out of control. People considered her nonconformist, maybe even quirky, but she managed risk by knowing her boundaries exactly.

Jake nodded to the bailiff, who asked the room to rise. Jake waved them back into their seats.

"Defense?"

Buck took his spot behind the podium. "Will you return to the stand, Dr. Keaton? That is, if you're able to continue."

"Mr. Collier." Jake had clearly had enough.

Maria squared her shoulders, needing no rescue. "I'm happy to go on."

"Why did you give the district attorney this ridiculous—All right, Your Honor, I'll rephrase. Why did you tell the D.A. that Mr. Butler had anything to do with his parents' deaths?"

"The law requires me to report crime. I had to tell the police when Griff confessed that he'd killed his mother and father." She paused. Wisdom required her to shut the hell up. Years of practice and caring for people in need ripped the words out of her mouth. "Even if I didn't have to report the crime, this child's in trouble. He needs help."

Gil straightened in his chair. Maria refused to look at him but swore inwardly that she'd do herself no more harm.

"Griff Butler is in trouble because of you," Collier said. "We've explained all the so-called evidence linking him to these crimes. They brought a grieving young man to trial on the strength of a lie told by a woman fifteen years his senior, who fought back after he ended their illicit affair."

"Objection." Gil's voice cracked across the courtroom. "At the least, the defense assumes facts not in evidence. We have only Mr. Collier's innuendo as proof that an affair occurred."

"I'd like to enter my client's journal into evidence, Your Honor."

"My objection stands. Maybe the defendant wrote these stories, but their existence does not make them truth."

"We disagree and we want the jury to have all the evidence."

"The prosecution has never seen this notebook."

Jake gestured for the defense attorney to pass it to the court clerk. "As you well know, Mr. Daley, the defense is not required to disclose. I'll allow the journal with the stipulation the jury understands no claims in this document have been proven as fact. The entries go to state of mind."

Maria watched it move across the room as if no actual hands were holding it.

"Your Honor, I've marked the passages where Griff talks about how reluctant he is to hurt Dr. Keaton by ending their alliance. He also notes the day she swore she'd make him pay for leaving her."

Maria sat perfectly still, hiding her shock.

But Gil had found his feet again. "...is testifying for the witness. Perhaps Your Honor could instruct him to wait until closing before he sums up his case full of lies."

"I suggest you both stick to the facts at hand." Jake's tone remained utterly calm. "Mr. Collier, have you any more questions for this witness?"

"No, Your Honor. I think we all know—"

"Mr. Collier, I gave you a break earlier. Are you asking for a contempt charge?"

Buck attempted a defiant look, but his squarish jaw wobbled. "No, sir."

"Thank you. Mr. Daley, any redirect?"

"Yes." Gil grabbed his notepad, but didn't even glance at the yellow pages as he stepped to the podium. "Dr. Keaton, did you have an affair with Griff Butler?"

"No."

"Did you read his diary?"

"No."

"If he claims in his journal that you were in love with him, or that you and he had a sexual relationship, will that be a lie?"

"Yes."

"Did you threaten to accuse him of murder?"

"No."

"Did he confess to shooting his parents?"

"Yes." She couldn't afford a second of hesitation. Her future did matter—desperately.

"Have you been honest in giving your testimony?"

"Yes."

He stepped back, flaunting his pleasure at ending on a rational note. "Nothing more, Your Honor."

"Anything from you, Mr. Collier?"

"One question, Your Honor." He danced with the silence for maximum effect. "Miss—Dr.— Keaton, do you love Griff Butler?"

Did he honestly think he could unnerve her now? "No."

Buck exaggerated his disappointment, as if he'd expected her to find the moral strength to confess her sins.

"Mr. Collier?" the judge asked.

"I'm done with her."

Maria looked at Jake. His gaze was troubled, and yet, a deep down kindness made him look like Leila, who swore he did not know how to care. About anything.

Leila had been wrong.

Like everyone else in this room, Judge Jake Sloane wanted to know if Maria had seduced Griff Butler.

THE NEXT MORNING, Jake lifted the collar of his black overcoat and yanked the cashmere collar around his ears. Normally, he hurried to work, certain he had the reins tight in his courtroom, but today, he didn't know how to be objective. He also didn't know whom to suspect, but the thought of Maria Keaton seducing that kid half enraged him and half filled him with dread.

He was ready with rage for a woman wrongfully accused. The dread came from his own confusing attraction to Maria, who'd ducked his every approach. He might not be the only man in town, but he had a mirror. He was okay to look at.

He had a good job. The evidence informed him women found him attractive. Since he'd finalized his divorce, the available ladies of Honesty had offered comfort in his so-called loneliness.

But the only woman he wanted had shied away from more than simple conversation.

He shoved his hands in his pockets and shrugged, his collar now seeming to choke him. Maybe he finally understood why Maria had been so uninterested.

A flake of early November snow blew into his eye, and he yanked his bare hand out of his pocket to brush it away. Overnight the snow had covered the streets and piled up against the Victorian buildings on the square. With plenty more storm on the way, the sky was about as light as at sunset. Veering toward the courthouse, Jake had to pass the relatively new shops, all made to look weathered, in the recently misnamed Old Honesty Market.

Men in thick coats and gloves were swagging holiday lights from storefront to storefront while a woman watched, leaning on one of the cement posts that prevented traffic from entering the shopping area.

He sucked in a cold breath, but was it the air that froze his lungs?

Snow dotted Maria's honey-brown hair. She crossed her arms over the top of the pillar and rested her chin on her hands. A long deep-burgundy coat cinched her narrow waist. She lifted one calf, rubbing it against the other as if to warm herself, and Jake imagined walking up behind her, sliding his arms around her, breathing in the scent of her silky hair.

Could she molest a client? A sixteen-year-old boy who'd needed her as much as any patient in Honesty could have?

As if Maria sensed his near-savage need for an answer, she turned. Jake stared through the fat, falling flakes. She looked back, her eyes anxious as if she had something important to say. It was the way she always looked at him—

until she pulled a strange coat of touch-me-not around herself.

Was it that kid who stood between them?

She opened her mouth but then only nodded.

He looked toward the courthouse windows. "Are you going?"

"I can't stay away."

He walked to her. As usual, she searched for anywhere to go, but he refused to get out of her way. "Why?"

"He needs help." She grabbed the tails of the soft ivory scarf knotted at her throat. Matching mittens covered small hands that trembled. Fragility beneath her strength made him want to cover her hands with his and rub warmth into her fingers. "You could help him," she said.

He turned, but her hand caught his forearm. Hell, he'd imagined touching her for damn near a year. He'd talked to her for the sheer sensual jolt of hearing her voice.

She was a witness in a trial in his courtroom.

"I can't discuss the case with you."

"You can see he's in trouble. Just flavor your instruct—"

"Maria, do you want to look guilty?" He tugged her hand off his arm, but she wrapped her fingers around his, and he found himself tugging her closer. "You don't seem to realize your doggedness makes Griff's side of the story seem more plausible. Why does he matter so much to you?" He raised his face to the sky as if he were reaching from under water for breathable air. "Don't tell me what you've done, and stop incriminating yourself."

"You mean, stop helping someone who needs me." She tried to pull away, but her wrist ended up beneath his thumb. The ribbing on her thin mitten slid aside, and he could have counted her racing pulse.

"I cannot do this." He eased her away from him. God, she smelled good. He wanted to breathe her in. He wanted— "If you say another word, I'll have to recuse myself." He turned away. His coat brushed at his legs. He ached with frustration and need stoked by the brief touch of her hand.

"I didn't touch Griff. He was my patient, and he's a sick kid. You know how to see both sides of any story. Why can't you see his?"

How did she know that about him? He pretended not to hear, though the slow fall of snow buffered them from everyone else on the square.

He wanted to believe her concern was just that. Concern. But women could lie, even women whose seeming innocence somehow infused the air they breathed with sex. Especially women like Maria.

She couldn't control her anxiety for Griff, who'd called her a monster in front of a courtroom. She might be so driven by her own needs that she couldn't turn her back on that kid.

This case was getting to Jake. He yanked at his lapel. This kid and Maria Keaton had nothing to do with his private life. He'd once had a wife who'd lied to him over and over and expected him to believe her every time. Kate wasn't every woman. Maria wasn't Kate.

He had to reclaim his objectivity.

"Damn."

Closing arguments would start by this afternoon. They could have a verdict before morning.

And then he'd have to take a disinterested look at Griff Butler's story and at Maria's—Dr. Keaton's. One of them was lying.

If she'd hurt that kid, he'd have to report her to the Psychology Review Board.

CHAPTER THREE

TWO DAYS LATER, just past 2:00 p.m., the jury filed in, all staring at their feet.

Jake avoided looking at the gallery where Maria was sitting. While everyone else in the courtroom had wondered if Maria was guilty, she'd studied the jurors with a pleading face, as if she could will them to see Griff through her eyes, as a sick child.

A sick child might not survive prison.

Jake gripped his chair arms, but somehow, he was remembering the silky seduction of Maria's skin beneath his fingers. He had to stop thinking about her. Her self-destructive refusal to back down reinforced his career-long commitment to keeping his personal feelings out of the courtroom.

He'd heard the gossip. As Buck had said, Maria's practice was anything but traditional. Apparently, she didn't believe in the conventional therapist's tools—a couch, a knowing smile, a "How did that make you feel?"

The obvious question nagged at him. How big a jump was it from meditating on mountains to making so-called love in her office?

Jake had to read that journal. Forcing his attention from Maria's face, he dragged his mind back to the task at hand.

The jurors sat. Jake nodded to their foreman. "Have you reached a verdict?"

"Yes, Your Honor," she said.

"Bailiff?"

The uniformed officer took the verdict slip from the foreman and handed it to Jake. He opened it, glanced over it. It wasn't a total shock. But, completely out of character, all he could think was that he had to decide what to do next about Maria.

Jake handed the slip back to the bailiff, who returned it to the foreman, a woman old enough to harbor grandmotherly sentiments toward Griff. She unfolded the paper and cleared her throat before she gave the boy a warm smile.

"In the matter of the Commonwealth versus Griffin Samuel Butler, on the first count of first-degree murder, in the murder of Channing Butler, we find the defendant not guilty."

Voices surged like background sounds in a

movie. Half the gallery agreed with the verdict. Half definitely did not.

The foreman continued, "On the second count of first-degree murder, in the murder of Ada Butler, we find the defendant not guilty."

Griff looked stunned, as if he'd been imagining prison walls and found himself transported out of this musty room to the middle of fresh new snow and the twinkling lights blinking holiday colors on the square. That kid had plenty to be grateful for.

Jake picked up his gavel. Conversation ceased except for muffled sobbing as he turned to face the jury.

"Thank you for your service to the Commonwealth," Jake said. "You may speak to the press if you wish. If you prefer not to discuss this case or the verdict, follow the bailiff, and he'll escort you to an alternate exit."

He turned to Griff, who'd reached behind him, turning over his chair as he grabbed at his family.

His aunt, still crying, held out her arms. His uncle extended a strong hand. Griff tried to take both.

Far from gloating, as the guilty tended to do when they got off, he just looked like a kid. Happy to be going home to the people he was supposed to love.

Supposed to. That was the problem. No matter what a man might see in his job, day in and day out, he assumed a sixteen-year-old kid loved his mother and dad.

At least Jake assumed. And unless Griff was adept at a sociopath's crocodile tears, he was grateful and glad to wrap trembling arms around his aunt and uncle.

Jake searched for Maria. Perched on the edge of her seat, her hands folded in her lap, she might have looked the part of a prim schoolmarm, but Jake felt a grim compulsion to get her out of here before anyone else saw how deeply she cared for the kid who'd thrown her to the wolves.

It was surreal being one of two still people in a room boiling with activity. Usually, a verdict freed Jake of responsibility. His job stopped at making sure the defendant got a fair trial.

Not this time. Juries were made up of humans. For the first time, he allowed himself to contemplate the possibility that twelve humans had made a mistake.

That skinny boy might have taken the gun from his father's safe and loaded the shells. Gil Daley theorized Griff had then walked up two twisting flights of stairs in his right-side-of-

Honesty house and stood over his sleeping parents. He'd had all that time to rethink his plan. Could a kid kill his parents because they'd grounded him?

What about his aunt and uncle? Jake studied the last two adults in the Butler family. With their arms around Griff and each other, they still reached with outstretched fingers, seeking even more contact, as if they all feared a cop was going to show up and drag Griff back to his cell.

Angela Hammond had lost her sister. Were she and her husband covering for Griff because he was all that remained of his mother?

Gil hadn't found the least whiff of violence in the Butler household. However, at the high school, the teachers and principal had described several escalating incidents, from shoving in the hall to a more dangerous infraction in the boys' room, when Griff had shoved a freshman's head into the toilet.

Which any kid might do if his therapist were abusing him.

Jake straightened, searching inwardly for his customary sense of justice served. Time and the law moved forward, and Jake had no choice. The jury's decision ruled.

"Mr. Butler, you are free to go."

Shouting and laughter clashed. A couple of groans layered in an undertone. The boy and his relatives started hugging all over again, still stunned and even happier.

Holding his gavel loosely in his hands, Jake eyed Griff Butler with Maria's doubt, but Griff was oblivious. He wriggled toward the aisle, past his attorneys, but then he saw Maria.

She leaned toward the kid, her face vulnerable, soft with concern.

She opened her mouth, as if to speak. Jake almost lifted his hand, to warn her. Griff's aunt saw her nephew's confusion, and she spun, a look of chilling rage freezing her face.

Maria stared at Angela, her eyes soft with pity. Jake swore silently as Angela's mouth straightened into a bitter slash. He didn't have to read lips to guess at the words she spit at Maria. David, her husband, regarded his wife with the dismay of a man confronting a stranger.

Maria stood her ground—sat it—without wavering. David gathered Angela and Griff into his arms and dragged them toward the exit.

The fight seeped out of Maria. She lowered her head as if she couldn't hold it up. Her shoulders hunched. Light glittered in the curls that framed her pale cheeks.

Her air of submission startled Jake more than

any other move she'd made. He slammed the gavel onto its rest. "Court dismissed."

He turned to the doors behind him and the bailiff, a friend since the first time Jake had defended a client in this building, opened the door.

"Over at last, sir," he said.

"Yeah, Joe."

"You should go out that back way, too. Those guys are going to want your opinion on the verdict."

"I have no opinion, Joe." It was the way he lived. Objective. As Maria had said, determined to see all sides of any argument.

Camera flashes lit up the back of the courtroom. Some of the press had come from D.C. and beyond. Griff Butler's father had been a congressman before he'd resigned to make money building strip malls. Griff's arrest had made big news because of his family name, as well as the depraved nature of his alleged crime.

Jake would like nothing better than to go to his chambers, hang up his robe and spit the taste of this trial out of his mouth. Instead, he had to decide whether to ruin Maria's career and turn her into a pariah in Honesty. No one would ever trust her again if one of the town's leading judges believed she'd seduced a patient.

"What do you think, Joe?"

"I'm with you. The jury does all the thinking. That's our system."

So why did Jake feel as if he were trying to find steady ground with one foot on either side of a fissure? All his assumptions were suspect.

"I hope you're right, Joe." He must be.

"Don't worry. You'll do the right thing." The bailiff held the door and nodded before he went on to his next task.

In his office, Jake took a bottle of Scotch from his desk drawer. On a normal verdict day, it would have been celebratory Scotch. He entered a trial entirely on the fence, but he usually had a gut feeling before the verdict came in.

His gut had deserted him. He shoved the drawer shut and dropped into a leather chair that rocked backward.

He couldn't ask Maria if she was a liar. He had her reply. Couldn't ask her clients. He didn't know who they were, and how could he trust their answers?

He spun his chair to face the window and the snow that had blanketed the courthouse square.

Wait a minute. He knew someone whose teenage son had seen Maria.

Jake picked up his phone and dialed Aidan Nikolas. A businessman and a friend of Jake's since he'd moved to Honesty, Aidan had mentioned that Maria was his stepson's therapist. She'd also worked for Aidan when he'd still lived in D.C.

Aidan answered his cell, out of breath. Behind his harried hello, a voice on an airport PA system called all passengers to board.

"Jake? I only have a second. What can I do for you?"

A second? He resisted a damn-near compulsion to back down and hang up. "I have some questions about Dr. Keaton."

"Maria? She's great. Remember when Eli was so depressed? He depended on her, and he still sees her occasionally for what she calls refreshers."

"What kind of refresher? Why would she insist on seeing a kid after he was well?" Jake felt dirty and angry. He got himself under control. "Why should he still need her?"

"Insist? Did I say that? What are you talking about?"

"Just getting a little information. Why does she still see Eli?"

"He tried to commit suicide a year and a half ago, and he's in the midst of adolescence. He'll talk to her, even when he clams up on Beth and me."

"Okay, but why doesn't she wait for you to call her?"

"Sometimes she does, but depression doesn't make a kid instinctively ask for help."

"And she worked for you in Washington?"

The phone filled with airport noise. "What is this?" Aidan asked. "You heard that I had to fire her?"

"What?" The room closed in.

"Why are you butting into Maria's business? Is something wrong with Leila?"

"It's not Leila, but I need information."

"Maria's testifying in the Griff Butler case. What's gone wrong?" Again, the PA voice demanded that passengers board. "Jake, did you just ease me into saying something I shouldn't have about Maria?"

"Like what?" The years that had passed since he'd done investigative work had made him clumsy. Inconvenient attraction to Maria had nothing to do with his heavy hands.

"She does not lie. Is that what you're asking me?"

To hell with subtlety. "The defendant made troubling accusations."

"You mean, the guy who confessed he'd killed his parents and then decided he hadn't?"

"The guy's a sixteen-year-old kid."

"Who shot both his parents in cold blood."

"You believe her? I guess that's an answer." Jake took solace in the familiar law books, stacked wall to wall in his office. Nothing came before justice. Not even his own need to believe that Maria was not the woman Griff Butler and Buck Collier had painted her in that courtroom. "Why'd you fire her?"

"I'm not supposed to—"

"I have to know, Aidan."

Heavy silence stretched between them. Jake let it go on. Aidan would answer if he kept quiet.

"I was fixing problems before they started. When I hired her, there had been several incidences of office rage in the news, and investments are high pressure at the best of times. We tried her out as someone the staff could talk to, but I have a company full of corporate types. Maria encouraged them to relax, rather than stress. That didn't work with my people. They thrive on structure. When she left, it was more mutual than me firing her."

"I'm not prying into your company's business, but did she ever do anything you considered inappropriate?"

"Inappropriate? What the hell are you talking about? What's Maria done?"

"You're quick to assume she has done something. I thought you trusted her." Man, he felt like a jerk. He'd rather not help Griff and Buck ruin Maria's reputation, but what could he do, short of getting the cops to plant some undercover "client" in her office?

"I've known you for two years. You don't jump to conclusions without evidence."

"I don't know what to—" In the background, a man spoke Aidan's name. What the hell? There was no time. "You're going to hear this anyway. Griff Butler says he and Dr. Keaton had an affair."

This time, the silence from Aidan's end of the phone damn near blew out Jake's eardrum.

"Not a chance," the other man finally said.

"Because you don't want to think she might have hurt Eli?"

"She's a beautiful woman and Eli's a teenage boy. He developed a crush on her when he began to feel better. If she'd done anything to encourage it, Beth and I would have taken him to someone else and reported her. Maria pretended it wasn't happening, and she kept working with him until he saw her as his doctor again."

"She might have been oblivious with Eli. He's younger than Griff."

"Do you know what you're suggesting? That she preys on certain victims?"

"I'm not." He was. He had to, but— "It kills me to ruin someone's career like this because of assumptions that might be lies."

"Don't kid yourself. You wouldn't just be ruining her career—you'd be ruining her life. And don't move on this until I get back."

"What can you do for her, Aidan? If I think she might harm her clients, I have to have her investigated."

"She kept my son alive when he wanted to die."

"That's why I can't ignore the accusations I heard in court. She has other underage clients." He had to call the Psychology Review Board. "I'm *not* sure she's done anything wrong, but I have to ask someone to investigate because of kids like your son. For the sake of anyone she's treating."

"Don't jump to this conclusion. Take some time to get at the truth."

"Discovering the truth is an investigation. Have you ever been concerned about leaving Eli alone with her?"

"My God. Look, they're going to shut the doors. I'm holding up the plane. Call Beth and tell her not to let Eli see Maria until I talk to her."

He clearly believed in Maria, but even the possibility of abuse made him cautious.

"Jake," Aidan said, annoyed.

"Yeah?"

"I don't believe you want to do this."

"I don't, but I have a duty to this town—to the law."

"You could bend a little. Be human." Aidan's voice changed again. "Yeah, yeah, I'm coming. Gotta go, Jake. Think about what I've said."

Jake pushed the off button on his phone, his stomach muscles clenched.

He found the number for the licensing board and stared at it. No matter what he thought of Maria, he had to do it. His very weakness made him certain he had no choice.

At last, he dialed the numbers, but then hung up and stared at his own shaking hands. One thing he knew for certain. Maria Keaton led with her heart. He didn't even understand that kind of person. The heart could not discern.

Jake set the phone down and pushed the heels of his hands into his eyes.

"Damn it," he said to the room and the world and his own conscience.

Shoving his chair back, he jammed his phone into his pocket. Then he grabbed his coat and made for the door. The cold air of November promised cleansing. But once he was outside, he was just cold.

CHAPTER FOUR

JAKE BURST OUT of the courthouse's side door
and ran straight into Maria. She stood as she'd
sat, frozen, her hair whipping around her face.
She was holding her coat, but her fingers must
have been numb. The wool slipped through her
fingers to the ground.

He stared from the burgundy cloth to the
woman who'd managed to grab a piece of him
from the day he'd first glimpsed her. He'd done
the wrong thing. For the first time in his adult
life, he'd chosen to ignore responsibility.

He'd really like to blame Maria for his lapse.
Shouting *This mess is all your fault* would have
felt so much better than dithering over doing the
right thing.

Instead, he reached for her coat. "Can I give
you a ride?"

Her eyes flickered with barely a hint of rec-
ognition.

"Let me help you." He draped the coat over her shoulders. "You should get out of the cold."

She reached for his hands, and the coat dropped again. He looked down. Her palms brushed his, her skin ice beneath a fine sheen of adrenaline-induced sweat. Touching her was more personal than a kiss.

Her desperation got inside his better judgment. He forgot about guilt and innocence or responsibility.

"You have to trust the jury," he said, his voice feeling rusty.

Life came back to her face. She snatched her coat off the ground. "Whether he's guilty or innocent, he's in trouble, but you can still help that family. Talk to his aunt and uncle," she said. "They'll listen to you."

"What is it with you and this kid?"

"Not you, too," she said. "Caring that he gets help and no one else gets hurt doesn't make me a pervert."

"I can't discuss his case with you." Perfect. How many times had Leila suggested he come out from behind the bench and feel something? Now her wish was coming true, to a degree she never would have dreamed. Not only did he feel too much for a woman who'd thus far ducked any contact that didn't include taking a ladle from his hand at a soup kitchen, he also sounded like an idiot—an experienced jurist who didn't even understand the concept of double jeopardy.

"Stop saying you can't talk about Griff. You couldn't bring him back to trial if he hired a skywriter to confess this time."

"We only have your word that he confessed the first time."

She flinched and tucked her hands behind her back. "You think I lied?"

Her hair blew around her face. The wind kissed her slender, exposed neck. He wanted to pull her close and tell her he'd think anything she asked him to if she'd just let him explore that creamy skin.

Unwelcome passion could blind a person. He'd learned early in life to resist it, because it never led anyone to a rational decision.

"Jake, are you listening?" She backed away. "I feel as if I'm shouting, but no one hears me."

"You made sure you were heard. Can't you see everyone in that trial wonders what the hell really happened between you and Griff?"

"I'm not a liar. I wouldn't risk everything I've worked for if I didn't believe he could be saved."

"You have to put yourself ahead of that kid and stop making me wonder whether Griff's journal is the truth. If I wonder, so will the police and the Psychology Review Board."

Maria sucked in a breath. Her face flushed as she struggled into her coat. "Don't threaten me."

"You're in real danger."

"Yeah." She pushed her hand beneath her hair to free the coiling strands from her collar. He swallowed, relieved that she was too distracted to see what she did to him with a move so innocuous as pushing her fingers through her hair. She reached into her pockets and pulled out those freaking mittens, but gave up before she got one on. "A normal kid neither kills his parents nor claims he has. That's the danger."

Bunching the lapels of her coat in her fists, she jerked past him. A hint of sweet flowers and precious spice caught him by surprise. Jaywalking across the street, she seemed to have only one goal. To escape him.

She cut around the square, toward the Old Honesty shops. He couldn't move and he forgot how to breathe until, finally, she was out of sight.

Slowly, he turned in the opposite direction, fighting for control. A white square on the sidewalk caught his eye. Moving toward it, he felt as if he were trying to walk on legs he'd never used before.

He should have made that call. Griff wasn't

Maria's only underage patient, and his family wouldn't be the only one coming after her.

The white square was Maria's other mitten. He picked it up and glanced back the way she'd gone. Scanning the cluster of men and women easing between one another, in and out of the shopping area, he couldn't see her. He started to put the mitten in his pocket.

Then, without thinking, he lifted the soft material to his face. Maria's enticing scent made him want her. Bad.

Sweat beaded on his forehead. He shoved the mitten into his pocket as far as it would go. Too bad the town had no community lost and found so he could get rid of it without seeing her again.

FOR ONCE, Maria wished she'd hired a receptionist. She managed her own schedule to keep overhead down. But, on Monday morning, three days after the verdict in Griff's trial, she opened her office door to face an answering machine that was blinking like an angry, red eye. She'd anticipated cancellations, but deep down, she'd hoped her clients would hang in with her.

Dumping her keys and coat in the visitor's chair, she stared at the machine. Her neighbors were angry. Yesterday, she'd been waiting to pay for groceries when she'd overheard nothing good about herself from two ladies talking about her in the checkout line.

"She's the one." The woman clutching a quart of milk and a pineapple had nodded Maria's way, her whisper loud enough to set off seismic detectors.

"That poor Griff. You know, he was in my class back when he was in second grade. You couldn't find a sweeter boy." The second woman had sniffed. "Outsiders, you know? This town used to be ours. We knew everyone. Everyone knew us. When a family had a problem, we took care of it at home."

"The chamber of commerce insists we need growth. This should teach those young intruders about small towns."

"You are canny, my friend." The teacher had plunked a massive box of instant potatoes on the conveyor, choking out a cough as white powder wafted into the air.

Maria had pulled her cart closer, unsurprised by their concern for a kid from one of the town's oldest families. But they obviously hadn't seen Griff in years. They couldn't guess at the truth.

Now, she walked around the office, pausing to open the blinds before she dropped into her chair and swung around to her desk. Both Gil and Jake had warned her. Time to face the bad music and work on preserving the job that had given her independence and respect.

She'd given the practice her time and her hard-won skill, and she'd powered through the days, believing she could do some good. She cared about her clients, but she was also vitally interested in eating three squares and wearing clothes. Loss of income meant insecurity.

She'd been the black sheep in her family because she was the one who accepted responsibility. Images from the past clicked through her mind like frames in a movie. Her mother's "friends," all male, moving into one of their temporary homes for what had amounted to extended sleepovers. Her mother's never-ending search for a new hometown and a new friend. Maria's sister Bryony's progress down their mother's blazed trail.

Maria had barely been out of middle school when Bryony had graduated from senior high. But even then, she could see that—like their mom—Bryony had never been careful enough when she gave her body or her heart.

Instead of clinging to sanity and each other, the sisters had argued constantly. Bryony wanted the same things that made their mother feel safe, while Maria had never craved security in some guy's arms.

As Maria had worked her way through school, Bryony had crashed with her between what she termed "life episodes." Maria had tried over and over to persuade Bryony she could be healthy and whole without a man. She had taken Maria's concern for disapproval and often suggested she wasn't Maria's personal psychological lab rat.

In the end, their mother had descended on Maria's tiny college apartment to referee the fight. The three of them had eventually forged a tentative truce that reminded them they were family, but Maria still believed a woman should only rely on herself. When Bryony had announced she'd rented a friend's RV and had begun working as a clown at children's parties, Maria had sincerely congratulated her on following what Bryony said was a "calling."

If only her mother and Bryony could see Maria now. They were too kind to enjoy the last laugh, but Maria wouldn't have blamed them. All those years of preaching caution and respectability. All that sensible life she'd lived.

A tight sob nearly escaped her throat. Panic. Before she listened to her voice mail, she sent an e-mail to her mother, begging off Thanksgiving dinner. She couldn't face her family yet. That done, she hit the play button on her answering machine.

"Dr. Keaton? Vince Dunne, here. You know, I've been seeing you to quit smoking? I gotta cancel my appointments." A female voice spoke in the background. "All of them," he said, sounding harassed. "Yeah, I told her. My wife taught Griff Butler in second grade." The female voice added something that sounded like, "Will you shut up." Maria strained to place the voice of the boxed-potatoes lady from the market. "Okay, okay, I'm hanging up," Vince said. And he did.

Maria pulled a legal pad out of the desk drawer and wrote Vince's name. Next to it, she noted, "All."

The next message started. "Dr. Keaton? This is Meg Lacey. I need to reschedule my appointment this week. You don't have to call me. I'll call you when I have some available time."

She wouldn't be seeing Meg anymore. She added Meg's name beneath Vince's.

Next.

"Maria, this is Beth Nikolas." Maria had treated Beth's son, Eli, a couple of years ago. They only met now for the occasional tune-up. She started to write his name beneath Meg's, but Beth went on. "I'm just calling to make sure you're okay. Call me. Better yet, come by for dinner. And friendship."

Maria stopped the machine to lean her forehead on her fist. If only everyone could see she'd meant no harm. And by "everyone," she did not mean Jake Sloane.

SATURDAY, MARIA SLEPT LATE, trying to shake the hangover of losing one client after another. Maybe vodka would have helped, or at least some Christmas mulled wine, she thought as she stepped through her front door to find hers was the only house in her modest neighborhood that didn't sparkle with lights and wire reindeer and giant Santas in snowglobes.

She wouldn't mind a portly Santa nodding wisely in her front window, if the budget allowed. She scooped the paper off the sidewalk. Fortunately, it still cost only a quarter.

Maria started back up the sidewalk as a car veered into her driveway, crunching snow and the sand the county trucks had spewed even onto side roads like hers. She steeled herself. Wasn't it enough for clients to call the office to fire her?

A blond woman with a sweet smile and warm eyes waved a gloved hand through her window. Beth Nikolas parked and jumped out.

"I figured if you weren't going to call back, I'd better come by," she said.

Maria tried to come up with a good story, but

gave up and went for the truth. "I thought you might have reconsidered."

"I understand. The phones have been busy at work?"

"You don't have to be my friend, Beth."

"No one believes you seduced Griff Butler, Maria."

"A lot of people believe. I don't have many clients left."

Beth crossed the yard and hugged her tight. "I'm positive my son is healthy because of you."

"Because he worked to get healthy. And don't underestimate what you and Aidan do for him."

"He had that crush on you, and I never thought for a second that you'd do anything to encourage him."

"People mistake gratitude for something more sometimes, when they're getting better, but it doesn't mean anything dangerous until someone needs an alternative theory at a murder trial."

"I saw you with Jake Sloane on the square after the verdict."

Maria's pulse went into overdrive. She turned toward the front door, concentrating on her paper. "I was still hoping someone would see Griff needed help, and he might have been able to persuade Griff's aunt and uncle to talk to someone."

"You looked half out of your mind, and he seemed concerned for you."

Maria ached at the memory of Jake holding her close. How she'd wanted to lean into him. "He suggested I stop worrying about Griff. Want some coffee?"

"Jake didn't threaten you with an investigation?"

Maria's stomach dropped like a stone as she recalled his words *If I wonder, so will the police and the Psychology Review Board.* "Is he investigating me?"

"I don't know." Beth took the door and waited as Maria tried to plant one foot in front of the other. "As you mentioned, I've heard gossip. People know you treated Eli, so they try to ask Aidan and me about you, but I haven't heard anything specific about Jake. I didn't realize you knew him so well."

It wasn't just that she didn't want even Beth to know she'd been daydreaming about Jake from afar. If it came out that she was treating Leila, she didn't want anyone to think she'd been unprofessional with the girl's father.

"I hardly know Jake at all."

"That wasn't what I thought as I watched you." Beth shut the door.

"Do we have to talk about Jake Sloane?" She

sighed noisily. "Or Griff? I could use a change of subject." She'd never make a good actress, but Beth took the hint anyway.

"Let's talk about dinner next Saturday. Maybe by then you'll want to join us. We can watch Eli on the half-pipe Aidan built for him, and you can talk to me while I cook. Then we'll fight for the best spots in front of the TV while we make the men clean."

Maria's first instinct was to plunge her head into the nearest pile of sand, but if someone in her situation had come to her as a client, she'd have cautioned against wallowing in a safety net of invisibility.

"Thanks, Beth. I'd like that a lot." She stood back. "Would you like a—" she glanced down the hall toward the kitchen "—something?"

Beth chuckled. "I've arrived in time. You don't even know what you have to eat or drink?"

"It's been rough. People seem to be lining up on Griff's side or mine."

"For once, I can offer you good advice. Don't hide out here." Beth hugged her again and then inched toward the door. "I'm going to skip your generous offer of 'something.' I have errands to run and several guests arriving at the lodge tonight to get in some last-minute fishing before the holidays."

Maria walked her back onto the small, covered porch. "Thanks for the pep talk. What can I bring Saturday?"

"Aidan likes your sweet-potato soufflé," Beth said.

"Perfect." Sweet potatoes and brown sugar wouldn't deplete her small bank account too much. "And what time should I show up?"

"Early is good." Beth patted her shoulder. "Try not to worry. The rats will swim back to the ship."

Maria laughed for what felt like the first time since the trial had ended. "I know you grew up with Griff's mother and aunt, but thanks for being on my side, too, Beth."

"You didn't know you could count on us?" Beth started toward the sidewalk. "Thanks to you, my son acts like any normal teen. He doesn't lurk in his room. He gets angry with me and resents Aidan and loves his baby sister." She peered back, her hair flying in the cold wind. "My child is interested in life because you treated him. You are a hero at our house." Beth lifted her hand in a brief wave. "Bad stuff fades if you wait it out. Isn't that what you told Eli?"

"I just needed someone to remind me. See you next Saturday."

LEILA HAD stood him up again. From his colorful red chair in La Fiesta's window, Jake watched a crew arguing over dead bulbs as they strung the last of the holiday twinkle lights in the market.

He checked his watch. Also dead. Then he pulled out his phone to see the time. He got a jolt as he read the ID of a missed caller. The Psychology Review Board. He'd dialed them and finally gone as far as letting the phone ring before hanging up.

Nice. Grown man so distracted by a need for sex that he'd betrayed the rules he lived by—do the right thing. Don't sway justice. Don't cheat on your wife. Don't abandon your daughter to day care and teenage angst. Be objective and do the right thing, even when it hurts.

Calling the review board had hurt. This time, doing the right thing could destroy someone else. Maria's practice might not survive investigation. At least in Honesty.

A sudden movement caught Jake's eye. Outside, halting so suddenly her scarf lifted in the cold breeze to touch her face, was Maria. She was tired, and weariness only made her look more fragile. The sweet curve of her mouth made him drop the phone.

She took a deep breath and pulled her mittens

out of her coat pocket. He felt hot as he recalled furtively shoving the dropped one in her mailbox after a visit to his Aunt Helen, who lived in Maria's neighborhood. Maria watched him, with a kind of hungry concentration that reflected all his desire for her. Shaking her head, she plunged into the crowd on the street and walked away from him.

He picked up his phone. There was the board's number—orange on black. To call, he had to push one button.

He pushed the off button instead and dropped the phone onto his folded coat. Why did he feel so damn guilty?

A FEW DAYS LATER, Maria was in her office, going over notes for her earliest appointment, when the door opened and a man she'd never seen before entered.

"Dr. Keaton?" he asked, looking official in a crisp suit, snowy shirt and thin black tie.

"Do you have an appointment?" Obviously not, but she was stalling for time to assess the stranger. The whispering that had dirtied her name in the past couple of weeks had made her wary.

"I have this," he said, pulling a letter out of his pocket. "From the Psychology Review Board."

Ah. Thank you, Buck Collier.

She took the envelope, willing her hand not to tremble. "Thank—" she started, but he turned and left before she finished. The ultimate show of disdain.

Instead of his face, she saw Jake's, his expression closing as all his worst suspicions were confirmed by this letter. She tried to see what Beth had seen—his hands on hers, his head bent toward her with concern.

She shook her head, trying to free herself. Wanting too much from Jake was no answer.

She peeled back the envelope's flap, knowing she was suspended, that the Psychology Review Board would be investigating Griff's accusations. She had to reach the few clients who'd stood by her, reassure them that they would be all right.

The letter was brief. She was ordered to cease treatment of all clients, and not to offer her services unless and until the investigation cleared her.

Despite her assumptions, seeing it in print was a punch in the gut. The paper slipped through her fingers, onto the blotter.

Her job was everything. Opening her own practice had assured her of a chance to stay whole, never to depend on anyone else for her safety.

She pressed her fists to her chest. This could mean her house, the car she'd bought last fall, the rent on her office. Her savings wouldn't hold out long. The desk clock, a memento she'd saved through countless childhood moves, rang the hour. Nine tinny chimes.

Her first appointment was due at ten. She had to start making calls.

First, she made a list of local therapists and called the two men and one other woman to ask if they'd be willing to take on some of her client list. Then she started calling her clients. She couldn't even offer to see them one more time, to ease them into the change.

She came to Leila Sloane's name. She'd tried not to let her feelings for Leila be colored by her attraction to Jake, but helping Leila find a safer way to endure the pain of her parents' divorce had also let Maria feel closer to him.

Leila said she'd survived on the outside of her family all her life. She had been the good girl whose understanding Jake and his ex-wife had taken for granted. They'd assumed she hadn't noticed the dark silences and the soft, cold arguments. They'd assumed the better relationship that had come with their postdivorce truce, with Kate living in D.C., had been as much a relief to Leila as it had been to them.

Of all Maria's clients, Leila was the one most unprepared to be abandoned again.

The young woman, barely nineteen, answered her cell phone. "Hey, Dr. Keaton. What's up?"

"We need to talk." That was a mistake. She couldn't bring Leila into the office. The suspension was effective immediately.

"I have some time now," Leila said.

"Where are you?" Leila worked at a day care in town.

"At my house. I'm off today, and Mitch is due any minute. We're going for a coffee, but I can try to put him off."

"No, that's fine." She wanted Leila to have someone around. "I've had some news today that affects you and all my clients."

"What news?" A wary note crept into Leila's voice.

"You heard what happened during Griff's trial?"

"Those ridiculous accusations Buck Collier brought up?"

"Naturally, the Psychology Review Board had to take them seriously, so I'm under investigation." Silence as profound as the grave thickened from Leila's side of the conversation. "I'm not allowed to see you or any of my clients until the board clears me."

"What?" Leila's voice climbed higher.

"It's nothing," Maria said. "A bump in the

road. But you shouldn't discontinue your therapy, and I have some suggestions for you. Doctors I've already spoken to."

"My father did this."

The phone went silent but Maria barely noticed. All she could hear was the drumming of her pulse in her ears.

Leila had finally confirmed what Beth had hinted at—the horrifying idea that Maria had kept at bay since the day of the verdict.

Jake actually thought she'd had an affair with Griff Butler. And, now, he was going to do what he always did—the right thing. Without even bothering to ask for her side of the story.

CHAPTER FIVE

JAKE RAN HOME at the first recess to pick up a file he'd left on his desk the night before.

But when he reached his desk, the file was nowhere to be seen. He rummaged through the detritus of last night's work and finally remembered he'd taken it upstairs when he'd gone to bed.

After a quick dash up the stairs, he snatched the file off the nightstand beside his unmade bed. He'd just made it back to the bedroom door when the phone rang. Late for court, he thought of ignoring it, but he hadn't ignored a phone call since Leila had moved out of the house in anger.

"Jake?"

Maria. He still hadn't made that call to the review board. When he heard her voice, and his pulse stuttered like a failing engine and his body grew heavy with wanting, he understood the depth of his problem. He'd never willingly taken a step outside of the straight and narrow, but he'd ignored his responsibility to the community by not reporting Collier's suspicions about Maria. Worse, he'd pretended he hadn't been thinking of her since the verdict. "Are you all right?"

"You need to call your daughter."

"My—Leila? How do you know my daughter?"

"You need to call her. Please don't ask me why, because I can't say, but you need to do it."

"Wait a minute, Maria." His thoughts rushed ahead of him. "Why are *you* telling me to call my daughter? How do you know Leila? What's wrong?"

She didn't answer at first. Indecision came through her silence. "Just do it. Don't overthink."

He wasted no time being insulted. "Okay." But he wanted to know, and Leila obviously wouldn't explain what was going on.

"I'm hanging up now."

"If she hasn't told me, she won't—"

Too late. The phone went dead.

A crash exploded downstairs. Thank God. He hadn't heard that sound since Leila had last busted through the front door eighteen months ago, shouting, "Mom, I'm home."

He reached the bedroom door in about half a

step. The file in his hand crumpled against the door frame. Nothing like an angry divorce to teach a man family was more important than his job. He tossed the file toward his bed and met his daughter at the top of the stairs.

"Leila? How did you know I was here?"

"Called the courthouse first." Breathing fast, she grabbed the newel post. A tall, lithe wand of rage. Damp strands of dirty blond hair stuck to her face.

"Why are you crying?" He tried to hold her, but she put her hands on his chest and shoved him so hard his back hit the wall.

"Why do you always screw up my life, Dad? Don't you have anyone else to torture?"

"Leila." He touched his chest as if he could feel the pieces of his heart that only his daughter would ever own.

Kate had insisted that he was as detached with them as he made himself be in the courtroom. He'd tried to show Leila that wasn't true, but he'd started trying too late. Her pain cut deep.

"Screwing up your life is the one thing your mom and I both tried hardest not to do."

"You talk a lot, Dad, and you pretend you see everything." Leila waved her hands as if she might be able to produce magic. "You see nothing. You don't even know how to pay attention."

"I don't understand you, and I'm a little worried. Maria Keaton just called me and said you and I needed to talk."

"That's what I mean. You're clueless."

"I am." But he was trying with all his might to get at least one clue. "Can you calm down some?"

Maybe she only exhaled, but it sounded like a hiss as the breath left her body. Half expecting her to shove him again, Jake stayed against the wall.

"What's wrong, Leila?"

"The first time I needed you, I was in kindergarten and you were my show-and-tell. I told, but I damn sure couldn't show because you forgot to come to my classroom."

"Forgot?" Once more, he rubbed his chest. He'd rather she'd thumped him again with her fists. "I never forgot. Are you sure I wasn't busy?"

"Mom said you forgot." She pushed back her hair, gulping.

"Honey, I think you're going to be sick." It wasn't a good moment to suggest her mom might have lied in anger. Or disappointment. "I never meant to let you down." He took a step toward her, but that only seemed to infuriate her again. "You're not mad at me right now because of something I didn't do when you were in kindergarten?"

"Are you really this blind?" She pressed

both hands to her face. "I shouldn't get personal." She looked up again. "Maria," she said. "Maria Keaton."

"I told you, she called." He struggled to make some sense of this conversation. "What the hell is going on with you and Maria? How do you even know her?" But as he asked, he began to understand.

"My doctor," Leila said, her tone so cold his blood seemed to freeze.

"Your doctor." He repeated the word, but he barely comprehended. "Your doctor," he said again. "Why do you need a doctor?" Images flew through his mind, his barely-a-toddler daughter laughing as she'd pedaled her tricycle like a guy in the Tour de France. A few years later, running to him with a bee-stung finger he was supposed to make all better. He'd always been the parent in their family. Kate had rarely been available. He'd listened to other men talking about their daughters turning into strangers, and he'd counted his freaking lucky blessings. His daughter and he had been through the wars in a dysfunctional family—and he'd managed to protect her from most of the battles.

Then, in college, she'd stopped talking to him or crying on his shoulder. She'd tried to stop needing him. "Why are you seeing a psychologist, Leila?" What was wrong with his daughter, who'd grown too mature for him to reach?

She misunderstood.

"You're ashamed, Dad?"

Maybe he'd become so adept at keeping pain private, he didn't know how to let even Leila see his true feelings. "Never," he said. "I'm sad that I didn't know something was wrong. And I'm afraid. How long have you been seeing Maria Keaton?"

Leila scrubbed at her tears.

"Tell me," he said, hardly recognizing his own ragged voice.

Leila lifted one arm, then pushed up her shirtsleeve. The blankness in her eyes distracted him at first. He couldn't see what she was trying to show him.

Then she shook her arm, like a talisman.

He moved closer, enough to see raised pinkish welts on his beautiful child's skin. Crisscrosses, like a pattern of tracks.

"Leila?" He felt sick.

She pushed back her other sleeve, and that arm was scarred, too. Jake looked her up and down, fighting tears of his own.

"My God."

Neither of them moved. He heard his daughter breathing. Now was the moment to fix things.

"How long have you been doing this to yourself?"

"You are blind, Dad."

"My girl." The words escaped him. For the first time in his life, in Leila's life, he couldn't stop first to make sure he wasn't saying something wrong.

Panic had him by the throat.

"Leila." He cried out for the lost little one who'd trusted him all those years ago with her secrets and her fears and the anger she'd since learned to turn inward. He reached for her, but she yanked her sleeve down and turned away. "Why didn't you tell me?"

"Tell you what?" He'd heard her tone before, when kids were desperate and afraid and grasped at defiance in a last attempt to save their secrets.

"I—" He couldn't think. All those years he'd tried to do the right thing for Leila. Apparently, he'd made everything worse.

"Tell you what, Dad?"

He could let her push him away emotionally, as well as physically, or he could wade in and try to drag his daughter to shore. "I don't know." He rubbed his mouth. "But I want to know. I'd like to help you."

She whirled away from him, her hair clinging to her face and her throat.

He'd been passive. She'd moved out after the divorce, refusing to talk. He'd tried to give her space, to help her by not forcing her to accept their new life until she was ready. Now he had to act, even if he only put his arms around her. He had to make her see how much he loved her.

"Help me?" Her voice was harsh. "You took away the one person who's been able to help me."

"Maria." He cleared his throat. "How did I take her away from you?"

"You did the wrong thing. Like always, Dad."

He tightened his hand on her arm but immediately loosened his hold, too aware of those scars beneath her sleeve.

"I didn't do anything." He touched her hair. "I didn't even call the review board."

Leila eased his hand away. "I'm not sure I believe you."

"I should have," he said. "I've been telling myself every day that I ought to, but I didn't."

"You actually gave Maria a break?" Her wide eyes pushed the years away.

"Tell me why you've been cutting yourself."

"I don't anymore." She faced him, toe to toe. The last time they'd really talked had been the day he and Kate had told her they were splitting up. "I wanted to hurt you, Dad. And Mom."

"Because of the divorce?"

Some of his incredulity must have seeped into his voice. She yanked free of him again. "So I'm nineteen. Old enough to handle my parents' divorce. Only I haven't."

Eighteen months yawned between them. Eighteen months of surface chatter and saying nothing that mattered.

"Your mother and I both thought you were okay."

She grabbed at her sleeves with her fingers and pulled them half over her hands. "You thought what you wanted to think."

And his daughter had been left with nowhere to take her pain, except to the privacy of her own room, then her house, where she'd sawed at her skin because no one could make anything better for her anymore.

"Leila," he said, choking, "can I put my arms around you?"

"No, Dad."

"Then prepare yourself to stand here and talk for the rest of the day, because I'm not letting you out of my sight."

"When was the last time you really saw me? I've worn long sleeves for two summers and you never even noticed."

"Maybe I'm an asshole." There couldn't be much doubt. "But I love you, and I won't let anyone hurt you." He went blank for a second. "Not even you. Or me."

"I always have something sharp, Dad."

His first instinct was to say, "Don't threaten me," but just in time, he came to his senses. "I won't let you hurt yourself ever again."

Her eyes closed. "This is pointless and juvenile, and I can see you're appalled." She began to breathe harder, as if she'd been running.

He touched her tentatively again. "I'm ashamed of myself for not…" *Knowing you at all* wouldn't comfort her. "Knowing what you needed."

"Sure. Whatever." She jerked away. "But Maria is the one who helped me, and I told her you were the one who set the shrink cops on her."

Leila should have been his only concern, but he couldn't forget Maria's desperate grip on his hands on the courthouse steps, her disillusionment when he couldn't give in to her pleas on Griff's behalf. His daughter needed him. He didn't want to care that Maria must hate him. "I didn't do that, Leila."

Leila stared at the dark wood floor. Her mouth moved as if she were trying to speak, but she couldn't get the words out.

"You can't talk to me?" he asked.

She half smiled, but her eyes filled with tears.

"You still look like my Leila." The second he said it, he knew he'd made another mistake.

Her smile was gone. "I'm not your Leila. I'm my own woman."

"But I am still your father, and I'd do anything to keep you safe." He rubbed his own arm.

She refused to look at him, but her hesitation offered hope, as she seemed caught between running away and needing to stay. "What happened with you and Mom?"

He couldn't tell her that her mother had only one hobby—other men. When Leila was forty-five, protecting her would still be his responsibility. "I want to give you something that makes sense, but we stopped loving each other. I don't know how that happens." And even pretending it had been that simple made him feel like an idiot.

"You fell out of love, so a divorce was my high school graduation present."

Actually, it had been Kate's. The day he'd come home and found Kate and her latest in his bed, he'd wanted to throw her and her skinny-assed lover through the nearest window. The only thing that had kept Kate out of a windshield and him out of prison was the inescapable fact that Leila would have had to learn the truth about her mother.

He and Kate had stuck together for several

more foul months, thinking Leila didn't need the added stress of a divorce before she graduated, and that after, she'd be mature enough to take a version of the truth. By unspoken agreement, they'd never explained her mother was a serial cheater.

"We couldn't live together any longer." Nothing he'd ever said to her was more true.

"Mom stopped loving you because you stopped coming home."

"Did she?" Any man would defend himself, but he couldn't. He'd accept all the blame. Whatever it took to stop Leila from hurting herself and keep her talking. "I had a responsible job," he said. "People depended on me."

"Try to convince yourself, Dad."

"Tell me what you think."

"You and Mom made my life a lie for years. You said you loved each other every day. In the car, over dinner, when Mom talked to you at the office. And they were lies. Every time, for how many years?"

All he knew was that those words meant nothing anymore except when he said them to Leila. "We thought once you were eighteen—"

She nodded. "Old enough to vote, but not old enough to drink or get over a divorce. I still don't get it."

"Then talk to me. We'll sort it out. You can't ask me not to try, honey. You're my daughter. I took you to kindergarten. I bandaged your skinned knees. I made you mac and cheese when you wanted comfort food." From scratch, because he'd been sure those little boxes her mother favored would preserve her till Earth men colonized Pluto.

She stared at him as if he were a poisonous snake who'd reared up to strike. "Did Maria talk to you about me?"

"What?" Did she know about his attraction to Maria? If she knew how much he wanted her doctor, how would that help her handle the divorce that still obviously tortured her?

"She keeps telling me—" Her eyes filled with tears. She whirled and ran down the stairs. "Never freakin' mind."

He caught her at the front door. "Wait, Leila. We can find someone else."

"Don't you understand? I can't talk to someone else, and if Maria said you should persuade me, forget it. Let me go."

"Okay, but listen a second. I'm still only a few streets away from your house. Call me and I'll be at your door."

"I don't want your help. I don't want to hear what a great life Mom has in D.C. I want to know the truth about my own life, and I'm tired of feeling like a fool for not knowing." She grabbed the door. "I can't get over it, just because you and Mom have put it behind you."

"There's nothing more to say. Our marriage just ended." He couldn't make himself give her what she thought she wanted. Young women might want to hurt themselves more after they discovered the truth about a serial-cheating mom.

"Yeah. Thanks for that. Thanks for convincing me that 'I love you' are the last words a woman can ever trust." She stopped on the threshold, half in and half out. "And thanks for thinking you could walk out on me because I was eighteen."

The door banged shut, seeming to shake the whole house. Jake yanked it open again. "You can do anything you want, Leila, except pretend this conversation is over."

"Watch it, Dad." Her anger mocked him. "The neighbors will see us."

"I don't give a damn."

"Maybe I do."

He shoved his hands in his pockets while frustration beat a tattoo in his temples. "I didn't walk out on you."

"Years ago, Dad. You were invisible every time Mom and I needed you."

"When you say you need me, I'm there. I held you at the E.R. when you had stitches from that bike crash. I taught you how to cut a sandwich in sailboats." He grabbed at anything that might convince her. "I was in the audience when you caught your bow in your hair at your first violin recital. I ran all the way from the courthouse square to the hospital E.R. the day your mother's crazy dog bit your hand."

"Another trip down memory lane." She gathered herself with a tight laugh that reminded him of Kate at her angriest. "If you want to see me again, leave me alone. I'll come back when I'm ready."

"Not good enough."

"You're great at pretending everything's okay. Now you can learn how it feels to wait and hope your life starts feeling normal again." She started down the sidewalk toward the house she shared with three other college kids. "You and Dr. Keaton and I—we'll all be doing that. Thanks to you."

"I didn't report Maria."

Leila turned, her eyes widening. "I just noticed the way you say her name."

If he could ever pretend to feel nothing, now was the time. Maria was the only person who could help his child. "You haven't wanted me in your life for the past eighteen months, and I finally know why. How am I supposed to sound?"

"Bye, Dad."

Her satisfaction gave him a sick kind of hope. She must hate him to be glad she was hurting him. She still felt something. She sauntered away, her boots grinding up snow on the sidewalk. He let her round the corner before he tore into the house.

He had to get to Maria.

MARIA OPENED her door reluctantly. Indecision showed in her narrowed gaze as she peered through the sidelight, then in the annoyance with which she turned the dead bolt.

"Refusing to help wasn't enough for you?" she asked.

"I didn't report you."

Her wide, agony-filled eyes called him a liar.

"If you've been treating my daughter, you know I don't lie," he said.

"You and I will never discuss Leila. Don't come back here."

She closed the door, and he had no choice. He couldn't wrap his arms around her and make her see he'd never hurt her or Leila. And he couldn't explain that he'd betrayed himself by not reporting her.

As he walked back to his car, Leila's accusation rang in his ears. He'd done the wrong thing. Like always.

MARIA WOKE EARLY on Saturday morning after a restless night. That was nothing new; she hadn't had decent sleep since the trial.

But last night had been different. Dreams of Jake standing on her doorstep, proclaiming his innocence, had haunted her. She wanted to believe him. She wanted to believe there were at least a few people in Honesty who didn't think she was a monster. But she couldn't. He had been the judge in the case. He was always objective. He would have done what the law required.

And it broke her heart.

Sighing, she threw off the blankets. She couldn't lie in bed all day, feeling sorry for herself. She had a full day of cheerful distractions planned.

First, she baked the sweet-potato soufflé. Then she picked up the basket she'd made for her little sister. Maybe she couldn't be with her own sister and mom today, but she'd long been making a semblance of family in this town.

She'd joined Big Brothers Big Sisters soon after arriving, and she'd been matched with

Carly Dane. Carly's mother worked crazy hours, and her father lived for most of the week in D.C., where he found more work as a plasterer than Honesty could provide. Carly loved surprises, and Maria often brought her a small gift.

Looking harried, with her hair escaping from a loose knot and her hands covered in flour, Leah Dane opened her front door but kept it only wide enough to lean through. "You're not welcome here anymore."

Maria stepped back, gripping the basket. "What do you mean, Leah?" Even as she asked the question, she knew. Leah was another person who couldn't find a way to give Maria the benefit of the doubt.

"Did you think I wouldn't hear?" Leah asked in a harsh whisper.

Carly appeared, leaning around her mother. "Maria, I knew you'd come. You said you would. I told you, Mommy. Maria never breaks a promise."

"I have this." Maria held up the basket, eyeing Carly's mother. She cleared her throat. "It's just a plush turkey for Thanksgiving and some fruit and nuts. And a kids' movie."

Leah snatched the DVD out as if she expected porn. Maria's face burned. She felt as if her friend had splashed her with a flamethrower.

"Okay. I'll look through the basket first, Carly. You go back inside. I want to talk to Maria."

"Mommy, it's mine, and besides, I want to talk to her, too."

Maria forced a smile. Leah turned her daughter, gently, by the shoulder. "Go ahead, baby. I'll be there in a minute." She waited until Carly was out of earshot. "I heard what you did. I don't want you around my girl."

"I didn't do anything."

"Buck Collier says different."

"Buck?" Attorneys weren't supposed to get personal. An errant, pointless thought brought her hope. Leila might have been wrong about Jake turning her in. "Mr. Collier called you?"

"He came to my house, and that's already got the neighbors chattering at top speed. People in this town assume the worst if a man's only home when he can be and a woman's got to work till late at night. They know what you did to Griff. It might make them wonder about Carly, too."

A vise threatened to close around Maria's chest. "You know me. Carly really is like my little sister. I'd never hurt her."

"That's not what Buck said, and I can't take a chance. We don't leave her alone because we don't love her. We work hard so she can go to college and have an easier life." Leah came out and shut the door behind her. "I'd kill you if I thought you hurt my baby. I'd kill you with my bare hands."

"Any mom would." Maria could barely see through half angry, half sad tears. There was nothing to say. Leah's neighbors would love a report of the exiled big sister boo-hooing on the stoop. She wiped her nose and her mouth, blinking hard. Then she held out the basket. "I didn't put in anything that would hurt Carly."

Carly's mother stared at the basket, of two minds. "Okay." She tucked it against her side, still planted in front of the doorway in case she had to repel Maria.

She didn't. Maria turned away. She was halfway down the stairs when Leah apparently had second thoughts.

"Maybe we'll call you when this is all settled."

Just in time, righteous anger rolled back. Maria didn't have to put up with these ridiculous lies. "Have I ever done anything to make you think I'd hurt Carly?"

Leah looked as if she regretted speaking up. At last she shook her head. "But what would you do if she was your daughter?"

"That's a point." It didn't make Maria feel any better. "But I'm going to clear my name. I hope you'll believe I'm innocent afterward."

Her bravado didn't impress Leah. The other woman opened her door and slipped through it. Through the thin wood, Maria heard the rattle of one of those old-fashioned chains sliding closed.

Maria made a living by her insight. She tried to be a reasonable person, but she was starting to get mad.

LATER THAT DAY, as she drove to Beth's house, Maria searched for a way to fix this mess.

Leah had reminded her that any parent would be wise to take precautions, and their children were more important than a stranger's right to practice. But in the meantime, Maria refused to wear a scarlet letter on her chest. She could answer the questions when the board got around to asking them, but she'd be a long way down on their witness list. And what would anyone in this town think of her even after she was cleared? If they were all like Leah, she could forget a second chance.

After dealing with Leah, she was dismayed to find herself parking behind several other cars in front of Beth's lodge. Even though she might feel like a walking sore thumb, Beth ran a fishing lodge. None of her guests would know Maria, and they wouldn't have heard the stories.

Unless, of course, they watched the more salacious tabloid programs.

Maria stared at the house, bemused about
whether to run or face it. She'd faced plenty of
stink eye since the trial.

Her body answered for her. Without letting
herself overanalyze, she locked her car and
marched up the stacked stone steps to Beth's
rustic door. Beth answered the bell, already
reaching for Maria as she opened up.

"I was afraid you'd change your mind," she
said.

Maria felt as if her legs were wobbling. She
swallowed instead of answering, and Beth just
laughed as she hugged her.

"Beware the apron." It was spattered with a
smashed cherry and several different colored
sauces. "I'm not a great cook, but you knew
what you were letting yourself in for when you
said you'd come."

"She means brace yourself." Aidan, tall and
handsome, swung out of the dining room. Also
smelling of spice, he hugged Maria, too. "We'll
be plying the table with antacid for dessert."

His wife gave him a less than enthusiastic look.
"Maria?"

Jake.

She looked over Aidan's shoulder. There Jake

was, taller than Aidan, more serious. The perfectly groomed judge had sleepy eyes and the slightest shadow of a beard. He wasn't sleeping, and something had upset him. Was he plagued by a guilty conscience because he'd ruined her life?

She couldn't ask him that in front of everyone, so she turned on Beth instead. "Why did you do this?"

"Do what?" Beth looked sincerely mystified. "Jake, what did I do?"

"I pressured Beth to invite me," Jake said. "So I could see you."

Beth and Aidan spun out of focus. Maria might have been alone with Jake. She might have blurted the question that had haunted her dreams, if she could have spoken at all.

"We need to talk," he said.

She nodded, still unable to find her voice. It mattered to her. She didn't want him to be the one who'd probably ended her career.

"We have an office." Beth pointed through the small living room. "You know where it is, Maria. Everyone else is in the kitchen, and we'll keep them distracted."

"Thanks." Maria led the way to the cozy, shelf-lined room. Heat from the fireplace made her claustrophobic. None of the fat leather chairs beckoned enough to make her sit.

She turned as Jake shut the door. "Was it you?"

"I didn't report you." Regret twisted his mouth. He looked different in jeans and a white cable-knit sweater that emphasized his dark stubble and hair. He rubbed his eyes and his hand slid over his jaw and chin, as well. Finally, he met her gaze. "But I should have. It was my job to protect this town from anyone who might hurt the citizens, especially kids Griff's age."

Hatred took her by surprise, shook her as if she were just a rag. Fury, hot and spiky, stabbed her deep down.

"You're sorry?" she asked. "You didn't try to ruin my professional reputation or essentially get me fired from my job, but you wish you had?"

CHAPTER SIX

MARIA SHOULDERED PAST HIM. He reached for
her. His hand brushed her arm, her waist. She
felt as if she were drunk. Only too much of
something heady could explain why her feet
refused to work. Why the door had apparently
moved farther away.

"Don't," she said.

"Please."

An ache thickened his voice. She nearly
stopped, but for God's sake, Jake was ready to
convict himself because he hadn't tried to rob
her of her job. Her identity.

"I'm sorry you neglected your duty."

She found the doorknob and turned it so hard
she hurt her wrist.

"Maria."

He wasn't sorry now. He demanded she turn
around, and when she didn't, he caught her arm
and turned her. She stared into his face, and the

tension between them wasn't about the job or the trial or even the fact that she couldn't be this close to him because of Leila.

"I can't," she said.

"Can't what?" He seduced her with his fingers, stroking her arm, and his voice was husky with the same intense need that made standing here reckless. "Can't want me? But you do." His other hand stroked her cheek, and she shuddered.

"I can despise you for wanting to end my career, just because of some misplaced sense of duty."

"You are treating my daughter. You see me through her eyes."

She'd thought women only gasped in novels, but she couldn't help herself. She closed her fingers around his wrist, and urged his hand away from her. "Since she is my patient, touching you—" she wrenched away "—is the most unprofessional thing I've ever done."

Without letting herself look back, she hurried to the kitchen, where Beth was surrounded by faces that looked like blobs to Maria.

She fell back on instinct. Don't make a scene. Don't make this whole public mess worse.

To hell with that. She'd had enough, and she wasn't taking any more, just to avoid offending people who were glad to pass judgment without bothering to discover if she was guilty.

"Beth, I have to go."

The room and the people went silent. Aidan took the baby girl from Beth's hip. "Go with Maria," he said. "I'll look after things in here."

Beth walked close beside her until they were out of earshot. "What did Jake do to you?"

"Nothing. It doesn't matter." Her manners took over on autopilot. "Thanks for everything. I'm sorry to miss such a delicious-smelling dinner. I'll call you."

"I don't understand what's going on."

"You will. The gossip must be flying." At the door she hugged Beth tight. Over her friend's shoulder, she could see Jake leaning against the porch rail, one foot resting against a stanchion.

"Should I get Aidan?"

"I can handle him. Go back to your dinner." She'd never been a victim before. This was no time to start. "Go back to your guests. The longer you're away, the more curious they'll be."

"It's not that I think Jake would hurt you, but I don't understand what's going on. If you need me, you scream bloody murder."

Maria smiled to show her gratitude, but she felt better after her friend left her. She opened the door. Jake pushed away from the rail.

She met his gaze head-on, but faltered when she could find only shadows and fear in his face. Suddenly, he didn't look tall, dark and menacing. He was in need—the one kind of man, woman or child she couldn't resist. Except she had to. With small-town scandal nipping at her heels, the last thing she needed was any kind of relationship with the judge who'd presided over Griff's trial.

"You can't possibly need to say anything else." Maria tried to pass him again.

"We got sidetracked. I came here tonight to tell you I didn't turn you over to the investigators, but I have a larger reason for wanting to see you."

"No."

"Leila," he said. "I'm begging you to help my daughter."

Begging. That was a word that would shock Leila. It held Maria still. He hadn't attained a judge's bench because he'd been a bad lawyer.

"I can't help you or Leila. I'm not allowed to see my clients. The little sister I've been visiting for over a year isn't allowed to see me because her mother thinks I might be an abuser."

He flinched. "Little sister? I didn't know you had family in town."

"Big Brothers Big Sisters? I'm not the only one affected by this witch hunt. And you're a judge. You're supposed to be fair. If you doubt me, everyone else in town must be packing me up for prison." She narrowed her eyes to keep from crying. Where had all her strength run to? "That day, after court, I thought you might help. You seemed so concerned… I guess I don't understand people after all."

"I was worried about you that day, not Griff."

Tears hit the back of her eyes and throat. She'd felt so alone since she'd stepped off the witness stand. She swallowed hard and shook her head. "That might mean more if you hadn't said some other concerned citizen beat you to the punch with the review board. You haven't asked me if I'm guilty."

"I heard your answer on the stand." Without moving at all, he somehow retreated and became a judge again. "Unless you have other information you want to share now."

His mistrust, however reluctant, tasted bitter. "I told the truth about Griff and, thanks to that trial, I doubt the police are even investigating anymore."

"Probably not."

She no longer knew how to read people. He was supposed to fight for justice, but he was content to let a murder go unsolved. He'd acted as if he were attracted to her, but all he wanted was to save the villagers from the monster and to have the monster explain how to save his daughter. "I can't help you with Leila."

"I'm not asking for a transcript," he said. "Just explain—"

"I can't."

Frustration strung his body taut. "Help me, Maria. I don't know what to ask her."

She pulled the sleeves of her coat down to cover her hands. "I want to help, but I cannot betray Leila."

"What if you're betraying her by not telling me what to do to keep her from hurting herself again?"

Maria stepped up to him. "Have you seen fresh cuts?"

He stared at her, and she realized how much taller he was than she. Maria had never wanted to depend on anyone else, but as Jake's face grew more tender—as she felt not just desire, but a connection—she had to fight a compulsion to sink against his chest.

"I didn't," he said, "but she made sure I never saw any cuts. I'm afraid she'll start again without you."

Maria wavered. But even if she tried to point Jake in the right direction, he might not understand what his daughter needed. "You can't be her therapist."

"Neither can you, so she's alone."

"I gave her a couple of names, and I tried to make her see how badly she needs to call one of them." She wrapped her arms around herself. "With Griff, I had to tell the police because he swore he'd committed a crime. Leila simply needs help. I can't tell you what we've been discussing because it would be unethical. I can't throw everything away."

She'd worked so hard for her little house in Honesty, green clapboards and white trim, neat and tidy and almost too cozy and perfect to exist outside of a fairy tale.

She saw the bedroom ceiling of her favorite childhood home. It had been a historic house, fallen on less genteel times. Squares of plaster had decorated the ceiling, each one an Arcadian scene. She'd made up stories about each picture, but she'd soon lost those comforting squares. Just as she was going to lose the home she'd bought and painted and paid for all by herself.

"I can't do it—even for Leila."

Jake seemed to shake in front of her eyes. He touched her arm with gentleness.

"I'm sorry," he said, and she almost gave in. Thank God she couldn't tell anyone how to "fix" his relationship with his child, even if she'd wanted to. "I shouldn't have asked. I'm doing everything wrong with Leila—and I guess with you, too."

"With me?" She lacked the courage to ask what he was supposed to be doing with her. He thought she might be guilty. She couldn't get that idea out of her head. "Did you read that diary?"

"No." Disgust made his voice almost guttural. "I should have, but I couldn't look at what that kid said about the two of you."

He did believe Griff. She moved past him. Her car was only feet away through flying snowflakes and cold slush that seemed to work all the way from her feet to her heart.

"Maria?"

She turned. The man was a force of nature, and he drew her into his orbit. She stopped because he wanted her to. The connection between them made no sense and shouldn't be, but she couldn't help wanting to touch him, to hold him, to make him forget the burden that created darkness behind his gaze.

He glanced over his shoulder. His privacy mattered to him. He'd hate having even Beth's guests see him now.

The windows remained blank. Quiet filled the air. It felt as if they were alone inside the flickering curtain of white. Jake came so close, and his breathing was so fast, its warmth misted the air between them. He bent toward her, his eyes rich with heat and panic.

Without thinking, Maria put her arms around him. "If I could do what you want, I would."

He leaned down, convulsively pulling her close. Her lips brushed his cheek.

"I can't…" *Can't touch you like this, can't wish you'd put your hands on me. Can't want you so badly I'm frightened, because you aren't capable of the same desire.*

She couldn't say those things, because his body and his hands sliding over her back belied everything she believed about him. He was capable. He all but melted her with exactly the longing she felt to be closer to him.

Common sense clamored. Her instincts were all off. She was getting everyone wrong these days.

But of all the *couldn'ts* that impaled her on her own bad judgment, the one that tortured her most as she moved away was her inability to stop staring at his mouth, imagining his lips on her skin.

"I'm sorry."

She hurried to her car, jumped in and started it. Jake didn't move. He was lodged squarely in the middle of her rearview mirror. Needing what she couldn't give.

THE DAYS PASSED, but not quickly. Over and over, Maria relived that moment in Beth's driveway, wanting Jake so much that nothing else mattered, wishing she could help him, hoping that Leila had called one of the other therapists but unable even to check on her.

Something had changed between her and Jake.

On a cold morning, Maria settled behind the paper, trying to ignore her feelings about Jake, her concern for her clients, the ever-diminishing level of her bank account and the envelopes stacked at her elbow.

First things first. Jake was still out-of-bounds. He wanted help for his daughter, and maybe Maria even looked better to him because Leila trusted her. But Maria had to do what the prosecutor and Jake had suggested during Griff's trial. She had to save her own life. She was scouring the classifieds for work that would let her deal with her unpaid bills when the phone rang.

"Morning," Beth said. "What are you doing?"

Maria stared at the paper's Help Wanted ads. "Reading the news."

"Have you reached the society page yet?"

"You mean, the tiny column that records the comings and goings among Honesty's rich folks?"

"The notables, yes. You remember the dinner dance at the library tonight?"

"I was never a notable. They only invited me because I was a soft touch, but I can't afford to be touched at all any longer."

Because she couldn't completely oust Jake from her thoughts, she suddenly felt his hands, dragging over her back and her waist, imprinting her skin through layers of clothing.

"You're not afraid to come out and show yourself, are you?" Beth asked.

"Well, yeah."

"You aren't the first person in this town to be suspected of something you didn't do."

"You might be the first to believe in me."

"I might not be."

"You can't imagine how humiliating all this is." She was every bit as private as Jake. "Doing a fan dance with all my dirty laundry at the library is hardly my idea of a big night."

"You've paid and the proceeds will buy books for babies. It's a good way to show people you're still their Dr. Keaton."

Maria set the paper and pencil on the shiny, polished counter. She brushed eraser crumbs off the newish tan-and-rust-grained granite, installed only a few months ago. With each change she'd made, she'd loved her kitchen more, but if she didn't find a job soon, someone else would be enjoying the stone she'd dithered about choosing.

"I don't want to care what anyone thinks."

"Consider this your own therapy," Beth said. "Come to the dance and show everyone you don't sport horns and a tail."

"I notice you're not asking me what happened with Jake." She hadn't even heard from Beth since she'd run out on dinner four days ago.

"I don't have to." Beth's voice was muffled.

"You saw?"

"I couldn't help myself. We have a window in the powder room off the side porch."

Oh my God. "So you've already had a show. I'm not getting paid by the public exhibition, you know."

"Then consider the free food you can't afford to pass up until you get some work."

"That's a point. Work is beginning to look like an impossible dream. The hospital doesn't even want me to volunteer on the children's ward, as of yesterday."

"Older people like to be read to, as well, you know."

"I asked them to assign me to the geriatric ward," Maria said. "They suggested I return when matters are sorted."

Beth paused a moment. "People in this town can be narrow-minded. You haven't cared before because you went your own way, treated the patients who needed you and got good results. Now you see the other side of Honesty. But believe me, if you hide out, they will assume the worst."

"Maybe you're right. I can wreak the perfect revenge by asking the hospital administrators who threw me out to dance. And what about Jake? You know he'll be there."

"He probably will. But that's good. We had two city councilmen at dinner on Saturday, and they quizzed me pretty hard about what I saw— from the bathroom window. It would be good press for you to prove you don't have a thing going with Jake."

"Damn," Maria said, using about three syllables.

"Exactly. Aidan and I will stop by for you at eight o'clock." Queen of the timely hang-up, Beth clicked her phone off before Maria could say no.

Beth probably knew best. Having lived here all her life, she had less problem reading this town and the people who made up its quirky population.

Feeling stronger for having a plan shoved on her, Maria set down her phone and picked up the stack of bills. She laid aside the urgent ones to deal with first.

Several envelopes down, she came to the official letter from the review board. It covered more specifics than their initial desist-treating-patients letter. It covered all the possibilities—suspension, loss of license, the publicizing of her transgressions to other communities in the country as they deemed necessary to protect health and welfare.

The words jumbled and rearranged themselves. Maria inhaled, dragging air into her lungs.

Courage flooded back when she least expected it. She crumpled the plain white piece of paper into a tight ball.

They needn't have wasted a stamp. She'd understood her life was at stake with their first missive, that they would be quizzing her clients and all the local dignitaries to discover the depth of her depravity.

Maria headed for her closet to examine her low-maintenance, low-wow-factor wardrobe. Tonight, she should wear something scarlet, tight and minuscule.

Too bad she didn't own anything like that.

CHAPTER SEVEN

THE LIBRARY, built soon after the Civil War to house a collection of books contributed by every family then in town, glowed by the light of candles and pale paper lamps. The fundraising committee had decorated the conference room upstairs to make it look like a private study in one of Honesty's wealthier homes.

After dinner, waiters had swept the tables to the sides of a parquet dance floor.

Maria couldn't claim she'd done herself much good with her efforts to smile and dance and talk comfortably while she wondered who, among those she'd danced with or spoken to, was accusing her of what. She hadn't felt this way since her father had walked out and her mother had embarked on a life of seeking a man at any cost, but those days were long past. They weren't coming back, and they'd given her excellent coping skills.

Which she put to use, evading the mayor's large feet and his moist, balding head, which was about level with the plunging neckline that had seemed like such a rebellion. The dress wasn't scarlet or minuscule, but it was tight and the most provocative garment she owned. She'd never expected to brazen out her own alleged sexcapades.

The next song was too new for the mayor, and he suggested they vacate the floor. She thanked him and made a beeline to the serving table to ladle herself a large glass of punch. If only she could have packed a flask of rum into her slinky gown. Brazening was hard work.

She took her drink to the most crowded part of the room, the edge of the dance floor. Like any other staid fundraiser reluctant to "shake her moneymaker," she sipped from her crystal glass.

If the D.J. could see at all through the sudden, thick cloud of disapproval, he'd recognize that his spinning moments were limited if he didn't find another Tony Bennett selection, and fast.

"Dance with me, Maria."

She turned, her body already betraying her with a jump in her heartbeat and a distracting warmth that made her feel light-headed.

Circles beneath Jake's eyes appealed to her

greatest vulnerability. She moved toward him. He lifted his arms, and she tried to step back.

Why couldn't they ever meet on her terms?

"Dance with me." He gave her no choice. She was in his arms, swaying onto the floor, trying to slow her frantic pulse, before she could even utter a "huh?"

"This isn't the way you dance to hip-hop," she said, trying to force some air between them.

At almost the same time, the D.J. realized his mistake and found more Tony B.

"Relax," Jake said. "You've been doing a great job."

"I have no job."

"You look happy and innocent, and you've danced with most of the town worthies. Without even making their wives jealous."

"I'd really enjoy hating you."

"Maybe I'm a little jealous."

"What?" She stared up at him, aware of her own shrill tone and the heads turning toward them. Best to laugh it off. "I was looking for a drink, but you've clearly found plenty."

"I was looking for you," he said, his tone an irresistible mix of dark mood and confession. "I don't remember the first time I started looking for you when I came to a party, but I always thought I was too old for you, and then

I—" He stopped long enough that she looked up. A muscle jumped near his temple. "Every time I came near you, you ran away."

"Because of Leila," she said without thinking.

"My daughter believes I don't know how to get involved. Little does she know."

Maria let him steer her around the floor. She couldn't answer without giving more of Leila's secrets away.

Jake lowered his head. "Are you innocent and happy, Maria?"

The threat posed by the review board whisked through her mind, but she refused to give in to fear. "I am innocent. Happy? I will be after I clear my reputation."

"I'd like to help you."

"Any more help from you, and I'll be living in a box on the town square."

He laughed. His breath brushed her ear and her throat. Hot. Tempting. She shuddered and Jake pulled her closer. Sinking against him would be so easy. So damn good.

Instead, she freed her hand from his to press both palms against his chest. "You need to let go a little."

"And ruin everyone else's show?"

His chest was as firm as well-toned, male muscle could be. His lips, surprisingly full, disturbed her every time he leaned down to hear what she said.

"I was fine until you showed up." She had to think about her feet to keep them moving or she might have frozen in Jake's arms. "I was hoping to convince these people I'm not a sick, desperate woman who'll drag any male into her bed."

Jake's mouth set. She'd clearly pressed a button.

"I didn't do it," Maria said.

"I can see you're trying to face down the scandal, but I'd rather you didn't joke about the whole Griff thing." He moved closer again, threading one hard thigh back between hers. Her breasts flattened against his chest, and she had to remind herself to breathe. "Please," he said.

Please?

"Why are you acting like this? People must be staring."

"I want to," he said. "I've wanted to since I met you, but you ran away every time I saw you. I didn't know it was because of Leila."

"I hope to treat Leila again one day, so this is wrong."

"You're not a member of the court. You don't have to recuse yourself." As he spoke, his breath ruffled her hair, and she clutched at his shoulders to keep from falling. He was aroused, and he made no effort to hide it.

"You can't see the conflict of interest?" she asked.

He backed up a little. She missed the thrust of his leg as he led her toward the center of the floor.

She didn't dare look away from the worsted black material of his suit. Surely everyone in the room could see how vulnerable he made her feel.

"Do you want me to leave you alone?" he asked.

"I want to say yes." She struggled to be rational, even as her body betrayed her. "I should be staying far away from you. You still suspect I'm guilty."

"I never said that." She watched conflicting emotions—guilt, desire and other feelings she couldn't identify—play across his face. "But I probably would have made that call if I'd known you were seeing Leila."

"Let me go." She pulled away from him.

"You don't want to go." He slid one arm around her back so far his hand wrapped around her waist. She'd dreamed of his body against hers, longed for the heat and the hardness that made her reckless. Now she wondered about Jake's motivation.

"I was supposed to do my duty."

"Duty is out of fashion, isn't it?"

"Not when it means protecting my daughter."

"From me, Jake." Anger at the injustice brought a rush of blood to Maria's cheeks. "You're wondering if you have to protect her from me, and yet you want me to help you. Would you even trust me if I suggested a plan of action?"

"Leila trusts you. Not me. Not Kate." He twisted his shoulders. "Maybe we're not much of a mother and father."

"Stop. I can't talk about her." Jake's daughter felt he had no right to her emotions because he and his ex-wife had hidden theirs for so long. Her parents' secrets made her doubt every assumption she'd ever made about her own life.

"I'm going to lose Leila," Jake said, his hands tightening again. "Really lose her. You know what I mean."

Maria's anger evaporated. She knew she shouldn't say another word. She would be breaking every rule of her profession. But she couldn't ignore the naked fear in Jake's eyes when she had the power to help him.

"Leila isn't suicidal," she said.

Wrapping both arms around her, Jake lowered his head to hers. Empathy and need were coupled in a dance as confusing as the steps Maria took. She and Jake moved slowly, listening to Tony croon through the sound system as if he were in the room.

Losing herself in the dream, Maria slid her arms around Jake's neck. It was only natural to seek the heat at the nape of his neck, where his black hair whorled in silk waves. It was like making love without the final commitment.

"Thank you," he finally said.

"She only wants to—" Feel, was what Maria wanted to say, but just in time, she remembered she was letting emotion jeopardize Leila's trust and her own future. She slid her hands back to Jake's shoulders, restless as responsibility raised its head. "I've told you all I can."

"Give me something I can do."

She curved her hands around his face, lying to herself as she tried to believe she only wanted to make him hear her. "Patient confidentiality applies."

Jake turned her toward the edge of the dance floor. They stopped dancing as they reached the dense crowd. At a sharp glance from one of the hospital directors, Maria kept her head down and depended on Jake to lead her to safety.

A mistake. He startled her, opening a balcony door.

"It's cold." She held back, not caring about cold but very aware of a healthy fear of going outside alone with Jake.

"You and I need privacy." Jake turned her, dancing her in front of him as he urged her toward the curving stone wall.

"Are you using me to get at Leila?"

"Maria, I understand the many uses of a court order. I could find a way to get my daughter's records, without taking advantage of your feelings for me." He crossed his arms over her chest.

She arched, trying to put some distance between them.

"You think I'm holding you this close because I don't want you?" His mouth was at her ear again. As she trembled, he caught her lobe lightly between his teeth. His lips closed and he sucked, and her whole body relaxed into the shelter of Jake holding her.

Yes, he did want her.

He turned her in his arms, and his hands were not gentle. Curving his fingers beneath her chin, he tilted her head and stared into her eyes.

Tension built and stretched. If he lowered his head, everything would change. It might make her life so much better, or so much worse. She caught his forearms, uncertain whether she was pushing him away or holding him close so that he couldn't rethink what came next.

Just as the strain grew so taut she wanted to scream, he bent and kissed her once, hard. And then again. She shook, clinging to his hands. He pulled her arms around him, and his mouth grew demanding, searching.

In the dark and the cold, she felt as if she'd left her body, and yet her body's needs were driving her into danger. She savored the sweet heat of Jake's mouth, the demand in his hands as he stroked her, writhing her hips in a suggestive, lean-against-me, make-love-to-me rhythm.

Her imprudent mother must have given her more than green eyes. She must have passed down the will to be reckless when safety mattered most.

"Tell me it's just a kiss, Jake, to tide me over until life feels better."

He only laughed, as he learned her face with his mouth, as his hands revealed secrets her body had been keeping. "Are you afraid of what the feeling could mean?"

She felt a chill that had nothing to do with the weather. He hadn't denied that the kiss meant little to him. She pushed at his stomach, sighed at the strength of his muscles flexing against her, yet somehow managed to thrust him away. "Sure, you want me, but you want to help Leila more. You have to listen to her," Maria said, dazed. "I mean, ask her to talk first, then listen."

"What?" He wiped his mouth, and she imagined pulling his palm to her lips. He tasted so good.

"Leila," she said.

"Leila." He smoothed Maria's hair behind her ear. "I love Leila. I want to help her. But do you really think I'm here because I want the key to my daughter?"

"Aren't you?"

"I only talked about Leila because you mentioned her. I got distracted because I am afraid for her," Jake said.

Maria shrugged. "Maybe that investigation's a good idea. I don't seem to be a good therapist tonight."

Jake turned toward the door, but stopped, running his index finger around the inside of his collar. "I didn't get what I want. And neither did you."

She was still trying to breathe when he eased the door shut. She laughed, because she didn't know herself, and laughing was the only option that offered her a mask. She started toward the door, but her dress caught in the spindly branches of a short potted tree that shook snow onto her feet.

She'd never been so cold.

CHAPTER EIGHT

IT WAS THE SNOWIEST November on record. The Tuesday morning before Thanksgiving, snow flew as if someone had busted open a feather pillow and started shaking it from the sky.

Jake knocked on the door of his daughter's house just before noon. No one answered, but inside, someone turned off the throbbing music that had rattled his own home when Leila lived there.

Jake knocked again.

The house remained as quiet as a grave. It would have been more convincing if the little sedan she'd creased against the corner of the drive-through pharmacy weren't nosed to the curb.

Jake knocked one more time.

Leila yanked the door open. "What do you want?"

"Conversation," he said. "Join me?"

"I said I'd call you when I was ready."

"I can't go along with that, Leila. Something went wrong between us. You needed me, and I wasn't around. I assumed you'd talk to me if the divorce bothered you." He rubbed his temple. "That's a lie. I assumed you'd be mad and I'd notice if you couldn't get over it."

"It's not just the divorce."

"What else?" Nonspecific questions made him wary. They made any subject fair game.

"Did you and Mom ever love each other?"

He stared at his daughter, who could only be hurt by the truth, but Maria's words came back to him. *Listen to her.* He couldn't listen if she wouldn't talk. He had to persuade her that talking to him was safe, even if he had to start with a hurtful truth. "I loved your mother once."

"I'm not stupid." She looked at her feet. "You stopped loving her how long ago?"

"It wasn't overnight. You're old enough to understand how complex relationships can be."

"Maybe I don't want to talk after all. Leave me alone, Dad."

Another door slammed in his face. What the hell had happened to him? And why? One moment he'd been on the bench in court, minding his own and the people's business, and the next, his daughter never wanted to see him again, and he was putting on a public show with a woman who didn't necessarily want him near.

He'd started this mess. If he was going to get his own life back, he had to find a way to talk to his daughter. He had to make sense of what was happening with Maria. And he had to find out the truth about Griff Butler.

He did what he should have done weeks ago. He pulled out his cell and dialed the sheriff's number.

Tom Drake's assistant answered. "He's not here right now, Judge Sloane. May I have him call you?"

"If you would. Do you have my number?"

"I'll take it off the caller ID. Is this about a particular case?"

He'd added enough fodder to the local gossip. "No. I'd just like a word with Tom."

THANKSGIVING SPECIALS were already running on Wednesday when Maria wove a path through ceramic turkey platters and foil autumn leaves to meet with a human resources manager for Canon's Department store.

An air of holiday anticipation reached even the waiting room where Maria filled out her application. People hurried in and out of the office ahead of her. Some were applicants, others were employees with questions. All wore infectious smiles.

Recently unused to smiles, Maria got distracted and made a mistake on her application. She crossed out the wrong graduation date under College Information and wrote the correct year.

Would her interviewer assume she was careless? Or was approaching financial ruin making her paranoid?

The office door opened and a man came out. "Miss Keaton?"

She stood, a little anxious but hopeful. The day before Thanksgiving wasn't a bad time to interview. She offered her hand. "Good morning."

The man shook it. "I'm Kevin Herbert. Come inside. May I have your application?" He pointed to a plush chair across from his desk. "Have a seat. I'll need a minute to go over your app. Usually, my assistant collects these for me and I take a few seconds to read them and gather my thoughts, but today…"

She muttered something—who knew what?—and hoped she made sense. Smiling, he sat in his own chair and smoothed out her application on his desk.

Maria concentrated on not glancing at the scratch of ink.

"You wouldn't stay long in this job," Mr. Herbert said.

"I would." She'd lie until her nose shot through the wall of the next room to get a paycheck. "I wouldn't waste your time if I didn't want the position."

"The 'position' is sorting towels in the Home and Bath department. Occasionally, you'd have to ring up a customer's purchases." He flipped the application over and studied her education and experience. "And why would a therapist want to sort towels and run a cash register? Trying to get inside the mind of one of your patients?"

Sarcasm always started an interview right. "I need the job."

"Might as well tell me why you're slumming."

"Slumming?" His attitude sucked. "Is that how you think of your employees?"

"Of course not, but a doctor who can make your kind of salary doesn't wake up one day with a yen to do retail."

"I'm suspended right now," she said.

"Suspended?" He sat back, a smile curving his mouth as if he thought she was pulling his leg. "Like in school?"

She swallowed. The man heated his office like a sauna. And his amusement would turn to contempt if she explained everything. At first, she tried to couch the facts to present her side of the story, something she hadn't been good at in court.

But game playing still wasn't second nature to her, so she started bluntly. "Have you heard of Griff Butler?"

"That kid," he said. "The one who went to trial, but his doctor…"

He pieced the puzzle together in front of her eyes. As he leaned forward, his good-natured smirk faded. "You're that doctor?"

"So I should go?"

"You're in trouble because of what that kid said?"

"I'm being investigated."

"And my wife says you were making out with that judge guy at the library fundraiser. Not that we were invited. She just heard." Mr. Herbert stared in silence, but he didn't hesitate long. He set her application back on his desk then pushed it toward her with the tip of his finger. "I'm sorry, Miss Keaton. I lose enough business to those fancy new places over in Old Honesty. I can't afford to hire someone who's in trouble with the law."

"Not the law," she said.

"I don't care where the gossip comes from. Maybe I didn't know your name, but even I knew about you. My customers are more interested in the daily whispers than I am."

"Maybe you'd get new customers who'd come in just to look me over."

His smile actually held regret, which was a nice improvement on suspicion. "I hate to make your problems worse."

It was only the latest of three similar interviews. Trying to explain further seemed pointless. "Thanks for seeing me."

"Hope it works out."

"I KNOW YOU," the stocking manager at the grocery store said. "I can't believe you'd think I'd hire you."

No need to explain this time. "I can't make much trouble setting canned goods on shelves."

"Not here, you won't be. I'm sorry I don't have time to be more P.C., but tomorrow's Thanksgiving. This is one of our busiest days."

He crumpled her application and sailed it into a big dirty waste can. Then he looked her up and down. Ah. He'd heard about the fund-raiser, too. She might consider the consequences the next time she decided to writhe on a stranger in front of a roomful of people who considered her a harlot.

This guy might not look like a pervert, but he

didn't mind eyeing her as if he could have her right there on the oversize produce scale.

"I always heard people like you beat it out of town when they got caught. You'd find a better hunting ground in a different place."

Running the bastard down with a shopping cart wouldn't change his mind about hiring her. She marched into the front of the store, trying to remember she'd once had some dignity.

She almost skipped her appointment at the *Honesty Sentinel*. But she'd begged for the time on this Wednesday of all Wednesdays, and they had a delivery route open. According to the ad and the man who'd finally taken her name and assigned her a time to come in, all they needed from her was a car and a valid driver's license.

She approached the *Sentinel* building fighting her fair share of shame and doubt. She couldn't afford pride. Her savings had begun a disappearing act. The only way out was a job. Or ten.

She found the newspaper's personnel office. Filling out the application took mere minutes because they all seemed to be set up the same way, and she'd filled out so many in the past several days.

"Sit in one of those chairs," said the assistant who'd handed her the app. "Mrs. Fellner will call you when she's ready."

Maria sat in a beige vinyl chair and waited, her fingers twisting like a nest of snakes. A few minutes later, Mrs. Fellner opened her office door and came out, reading the page her assistant had given her. She took a look at Maria and then went back to the application.

"You're older than we usually get."

"I'm reliable, too."

"You understand this job means early hours? People want to read the news over their morning coffee."

"I'll be here whatever time you want me."

"For your route, the papers are dropped at the corner of Oak and Lafayette at four forty-five. Let me see your license."

Maria handed it over, even though the assistant had copied it and stapled the copy to the application.

"Be at Oak and Lafayette in the morning." Mrs. Fellner passed her license back. "You know tomorrow's Thanksgiving?"

Suddenly, she had plenty to be grateful for. "Uh-huh," she said, too stunned to offer more eloquent thanks.

"The current delivery boy will show you your route. Stop at Lisa's desk to finish your paperwork."

"Thanks." Maria offered her hand.

"Oh, yeah." Mrs. Fellner, already on the way back to her office, came back. She pushed her glasses up her nose and finally looked Maria in the eye. Maria quaked with a touch of dread. But no. The other woman shook hands. "Good luck. Don't make anyone call me because his paper's late."

"I'd pull them off the press myself, if I had to."

"YOU'LL BE FINE," Tommy Laycock told her the next morning after he'd tossed a paper into the center of a little Cape Cod's door.

"Nobody ever complains about you hitting their houses?" He had a precise arm and aim.

"Sometimes, the dogs fly out of the doggie doors and chase me down the street." He patted the tufted console between them. "I don't have me any cool wheels like this. I have a bike."

"I may be looking for one soon."

He heehawed with earsplitting spontaneity, but it was a welcome sound. "You're lucky. We used to have to leave envelopes for payment. Some people even stiffed me once a week with that stupid envelope. Then, about eight months ago, the paper finally started billing them from the office."

"So I don't have to collect money."

"Or break any arms." He flexed his hands, gave his knuckles a quick crack.

"Why are you quitting, Tommy?" His personality seemed like such a fit.

"I joined the band and we practice in the morning before school. There's a girl in my class. She plays the tuba. I'm not saying she looks good in that thing, but when she takes it off…"

"Never mind." It was the last conversation she needed to have with a kid. "Thanks for showing me the houses."

"You think you'll remember?"

"Sure. I wrote them all down." She dropped him back at Oak and Lafayette.

"Bye, Dr. Keaton," he yelled as he unlocked his bike.

She waved, surprised he knew her name. For a second she was tempted to ask if Tommy knew Griff. Common sense rescued her in time. She didn't need to know if the kid was all right. He was someone else's problem now.

At home, she washed the ink off her hands and fell facefirst onto the sofa, sleeping for the first time in weeks as if she weren't anxious about her next meal. A paper route didn't go a long way toward security, but it was a crack in the door.

Later, as bright sunlight crept across the

sky through her family room window, she opened her eyes. And licked her dry lips. She'd slept for hours.

Coffee. Coffee would start her second try at a morning well. Attempting a lousy whistle, she got busy, putting together her meager Thanksgiving dinner. A chicken breast in the oven. Potatoes, both sweet and Yukon Gold didn't cost much. Neither did fresh green beans or bagged dressing mix.

The phone rang while she was cutting onions and indulging in a good old reluctant cry. She wiped her hands on a towel and grabbed the phone.

"Hey," said her sister, Bryony.

"Huh?"

"How ya doing?"

"I'm fine, Bryony. Do you need something?"

"Need something?" Bryony sounded mystified. "Oh, I get it. You mean, why am I calling?"

In the privacy of her own home, Maria blushed. "I didn't mean to—"

"Nah, don't worry about it. I'm fine. I'm really doing well. Lots of children's parties. Clowns are even in demand at adult functions these days, except they usually want me to be my evil incarnation."

"I'd have nightmares for a month."

"I know, but it's all good to me. I thought you might be lonely today."

"I am, but I couldn't face—"

"Mom and me? But we wouldn't interrogate you. We both know you couldn't do anything wrong."

"I feel bad. I wasn't nice to you a minute ago."

"I don't get how this all happened, but nobody's going to believe you'd hurt a kid. They'll look at your records and talk to your other patients."

"Clients."

"Whatever. They aren't going to lie about you."

"Some of them are pretty unwell. What if the suggestion that I'd do something wrong gives them an idea that appeals to their illnesses?"

"You'll deal. Don't borrow that trouble." Bryony took a deep, loud breath. "Let me send you some money."

"No." Never going to happen. She'd beg in the street before she took a handout from her mother or her sister.

"You've helped me before. And Mom. Let me help you."

"No. Thanks for offering, Bryony. And for calling. I needed to hear you believed in me."

"I always will. I'd better go. I think I smell smoke from the kitchen. Happy Thanksgiving."

Her favorite holiday. A day for family—or for lovers, she thought, with memories of Jake dancing in her mind's eye. Thinking of him only made her feel uncertain. They'd both used his daughter as a barrier to feelings that felt untimely and impossible. It was no way to act about family.

"I love you, Bryony."

"Yeah?" They hadn't said those words much as children. Maria had tried to change that after she left for college. It still didn't come easily to Bryony. "I love you, too," she said. "Keep fighting."

"I am."

She went back to her dinner with a happier heart. She even turned on the Macy's parade in time to see Underdog taking to the sky. If a beagle in a cape could be a superhero, she could at least find the power to make a living until she got her career back.

"I HAVE ENOUGH for both of us, Leila. Please come home for Thanksgiving dinner." Jake waited, hearing only silence amidst the static on his cell. He'd invited Leila to dinner at regular intervals for over a week. She'd ignored his calls and the cards he'd slipped into her mailbox and inside the screen door of her rented town house.

Just as he pulled the phone away, she spoke up. "Stop calling me, Dad. I don't want to talk to you."

"It's a special day. Can't we call a truce?"

"No."

"I don't want you to be alone."

"I'm with my roommates, my friends. They're more my family than you and Mom ever were. They don't keep secrets."

"Maybe we were wrong, but I'll talk to you about anything now."

"Has it occurred to you that Maria's living without any pay? She still has office rent and a house payment and probably malpractice insurance. It's the end of the month."

"I'm sure she has savings, Leila." He said it so casually because he was so damn concerned he might be wrong.

"She's barely in her thirties, and she doesn't charge nearly what the other therapists in town do. I know."

"I didn't start the investigation, and I can't try to stop it. Even if I did, I'd make more trouble for her." Especially after the library dance.

"Maybe," his daughter said, considering.

He allowed himself a silent fist pump. Anytime she didn't immediately reject every word out of his mouth was a triumph.

"I still don't understand why you didn't talk to me first. Even if you'd wanted me to respect your privacy, you're covered by my insurance while you're in college. You could have gone to any doctor."

"Dad, you're a clod. I kept on seeing Maria, not because she was cut-rate, but because she helped me. She's helped a lot of people, kids I know, too, without doing anything inappropriate. She deserves more support from her clients and from the people who hold the power in this town. She's only lived here for two years, and I know she's done a lot of work on her house. How much could she have saved?"

"What do you want me to do, Leila?"

"Maybe you should take her that Thanksgiving dinner."

She hung up on him before he could answer.

"Are you kidding?" he asked his dead phone.

But maybe she made sense. Maybe Leila had just given him an excuse. He hadn't called Maria since the fundraiser. He'd felt embarrassed. She'd been angry, thinking he was seducing her to get answers to Leila's problems. True, he'd been grateful to get her help, but he'd touched her because he couldn't go another second holding her close and not giving in to long-suppressed need.

As he repacked the dinner he'd bought for himself and Leila, he admitted he wanted to see Maria again. And maybe Leila would give him points when he showed up at her house, covered in giblets, to report Maria had thrown their dinner back in his face.

After he packed everything inside the warming bag the store had given him, he somehow had cranberry sauce and yeast rolls left over. Instead of trying to work the Rubik's Cube puzzle of wedging them in, he took a plastic bag and tossed the sauce and bread inside.

Just before he left, he grabbed a bottle of brandy for his aunt who lived close to Maria. He took her brandy every year for the holidays. She had a heart condition and she could only tipple a little, so she made the bottle stretch.

In the car, he had to turn on the radio to drown out the warning voices that shouted he might be asking Maria to douse him in gravy. He wouldn't even blame her if she wreaked a little havoc. He deserved it for making a spectacle of her in front of half the town. Maybe letting her assault him with his store-bought dinner would be penance enough to prove he couldn't help wanting her.

He drove past Leila's town house. So many

cars were nosed into the parking lot that the sheriff and all his deputies would be kept busy writing tickets all day. At least she wasn't alone.

His aunt Helen wasn't home when he knocked on her door. Often, she and her cronies met for the holidays. At an age where several had lost spouses, and many of their children had left Honesty for more cosmopolitan pastures, they kept one another company.

Maybe making sure Maria didn't spend today alone might not be such a farfetched idea. He left the brandy in Helen's mailbox with a note then drove down the street to Maria's little green house.

Her yard was tidy, her paint fresh. He stared at the windows that looked like made-up eyes with their diaphanous curtains and drapes.

Her home welcomed him, even if she might not. Two years ago, this house had been a run-down blight in Helen's neighborhood. After it had been sold, but long before he'd learned Maria was the new owner, he'd driven past this place with growing envy.

She'd transformed it into a home. Cozy and warm—and probably closed to him.

He grabbed the dinner stuff from the backseat and headed up the sidewalk, his heart beating like a kid's on his first date. Not giving himself time to think about right or wrong, he punched the small, glowing doorbell.

The curtain nearest the door flickered. Then nothing happened.

He could ring again, or stand here like a neon "I'm the guy who made a fool of himself with the woman who lives here" sign. As if she saw it that way, too, Maria snatched the door open. She grabbed his bread bag arm and yanked him inside.

He stumbled into a wide family room, glimpsing scarred wooden floors and a few pieces of expensive chintz, overstuffed furniture.

"What are you doing here?" Maria asked. "Aren't people talking about me enough?"

"I could be a good cover for you."

"That's a hell of a thing to say after the other night—" She broke off as he grinned. "You're joking."

Nodding, he glanced toward the door. "I am. But maybe I should park my car in your garage. Or at my aunt's down the street."

"Helen's your aunt?"

The change of subject was almost too easy. He couldn't have managed it better if he'd done it with a plan. "You know her?"

"With the dogs?" Helen's Afghan wolfhounds were more like hooligan teenagers. "I didn't put your names together," Maria said. "You ought to walk those dogs for her."

"I've tried to get her to take them to obedience school. To her, they're just 'rowdy, delightful children,' and she can't admit the truth even to get help."

"They're a menace. She's pretty fragile, you know."

"I've warned her they'll break her hip one day."

"How subtle of you. I can't imagine why she didn't take your advice." Maria looked at the bags. "What's that?"

"Dinner." He sniffed. Hers smelled a lot better than the victuals he'd paid for. "But you don't need any, do you?"

"Why would you bring me dinner?" Pale color stained her cheeks. "You don't think the other night meant anything?"

He stared at her slightly open, shiny, moist lips. Maybe he could make her take that back.

"We've already established I don't pretend for the sake of politeness," he said. "It meant plenty, and you should admit it."

"Kissing you was a mistake."

"You wanted more than kissing," he said, restless, looking for a place to set his bags. "So did I. I've thought about it every night since.

And most of every day. Not even Leila could call me detached at this point."

Maria ducked her head. She clasped her hands in front of her and, when he wanted to demand she face him to admit she cared as much as he, she squared her shoulders and obviously faced her demons. "You should leave."

He clearly cared more. "Maybe we could share our food," he said, trying to be kind. "Yours smells better than mine."

"Please tell me this isn't about your daughter."

"Please stop assuming I'd treat you like that. Leila did suggest I owed you dinner, but I think she meant I owed you more."

"You came because she told you to?" She folded her arms but then let them drop. A slow smile curved her lips. "Wait. You actually spoke to her?"

"You sound glad." Fortunately, his hands were still full of dinner, so he couldn't touch her. They might have ended up anywhere but at a table. "You make me think I might not be foolish to hope she'll give me another chance."

"You must have offered her dinner, and she turned you down?"

He nodded. "I'm being honest. Does that count for anything?"

"Did you bring pie?"

"I ordered it with the rest of this," he said, laughing, falling a little in love with the light in her green eyes. "I don't remember what kind I asked for."

Maria sighed and ran her hands down the curve of her hips. He nearly dropped Thanksgiving dinner on her floor. "I like it all," she said, as if that were a bad thing.

He maneuvered both bags under his left arm then put out his right hand. "Truce?" he asked, feeling betrayed by his own husky tone.

She hesitated, a pulse throbbing at the pressure point in her throat. "Truce," she said, her whisper pure seduction.

She turned in front of him without shaking his hand. He let out a breath. If he didn't lose his job and his sanity over this, he'd be the luckiest man alive. He'd been so sure—of everything—all his life. How had he lost his way the moment he'd first touched Maria?

CHAPTER NINE

THEY POOLED their dinner. Maria ate bits of both, though neither seemed to have much taste. Instead, she found herself noticing the way Jake flexed his fingers as he lifted a bite of roll to his mouth, or his Adam's apple bobbing as he choked down some dry meat. Hers, or the store's? She'd lost track.

Jake carried out a more scientific examination, scooping first her mashed potatoes then a spoon of the store's onto his plate. His thoughtful sampling focused all Maria's attention on his mouth. "Yours are better," he said.

"I doubt it," she said, wondering why they were comparing the quality of each other's mouths. Remembering mashed potatoes was the subject under discussion, she felt herself blush.

Jake had the gall to look amused, though his fork shook as he lowered it to the table. "Did you look at the pie?"

"Pumpkin. My favorite."

"Mine, too."

"Yeah." He moved and somehow his plate leaped toward the edge of the table. They both reached for it, but her hand only covered his. As she met his gaze, she remembered how alone they were—and look how they'd behaved the other night in front of a crowd.

Metaphorically, she held tight to her sense of responsibility. "Careful," she said, trying to infuse her voice with something other than longing. "I may have to sell that china for food."

He slid it farther into safety. "You look more hopeful, Maria."

"I got a job."

He caught her wrist with touching happiness. "What job?"

She laughed at his surprise. "You thought no one would hire me?"

He shrugged, and this time they both laughed, not because anything was funny, but because being together was right. For now, Maria told herself. For now.

He sat back. "I like feeling comfortable with you."

"That's a big confession from a guy whose heart has never been near his sleeve. What do you mean by comfortable, exactly?" As soon as the words left her mouth, she knew she'd opened a big door that should have remained bolted shut. They had no business taking stock of a barely begun relationship when his daughter needed her, and Maria still wasn't sure if Jake thought she had seduced Griff Butler.

"I mean, I want you and I want to know you better, and I wish you could see it's okay to feel the same way."

Maria was no coward, but she hadn't jumped off too many cliffs—without a bungee cord, anyway.

"It was one dance and a few kisses," she said.

"And today. Dinner on a holiday."

"Don't read anything into that. Your daughter ordered you over here. She probably thinks you'll feel sorry for me and compromise your rather infamous moral code to get me out of trouble."

"Infamous?"

"*Fabled* might be the better word, but you're confusing me."

"If I came around this table and took you in my arms, what would you do?"

Probably give in to any idea he could spin out of thin air. "I might use you to forget my problems."

The first hint of doubt manifested itself in the ghost of a frown. "Are you?"

Hell, no. "I don't lie to myself." She managed a smile. "Though I wish I could lie to you."

His smile was all smug male. "I'm glad you can't."

"I'll get that dessert."

"We're still eating dinner, Maria."

She looked at his plate then at her own, still full of Thanksgiving turkey and all the fixings. The air snapped with inappropriate conversation. When she stopped to wonder why they were rushing toward decisions best left unmade, she recovered her reason.

"Why did you really come today, Jake? Leila gave you permission, but you don't do anything you don't want to do."

"I wanted to see you."

"Even though you half believe I slept with a kid I was supposed to be helping?"

"Why do we have to talk about that?"

She put her fork and knife on her plate. "I don't believe you're capable of looking at me without thinking of it."

"Because Leila says I'm so locked into doing the right thing?"

"I'm not breaking any more confidences. Besides, that's the one thing that's easy to read about you. I can see you didn't want to make that call, but you would have if someone hadn't beaten you to it."

"Around the courthouse I hear that someone was Buck Collier. See? You and Leila don't know me the way you think you do—I can even gossip." He stirred his potatoes, making them more mush than mash, until he seemed to reach a decision. "It's bad enough that my daughter thinks I'm cold, but I'm startled how much it really hurts that you assume it without even knowing me."

"Tell me the truth," Maria said. "Tell me the things you're afraid to say to Leila."

He moved so suddenly in his chair she thought it might fall over. "You think I'm afraid?" he said, clearly incredulous.

She wavered on the edge of another precipice. Digging for insights about Jake might be the most dangerous risk she'd ever take. Her heart ached for the distress that cut his face to the bone, but she didn't want to care about him. Reclaiming her life and her reputation had to be her first concern. She was no Keaton woman who let a man compromise intelligent decisions.

She rose to distance herself from Jake and his secrets, but he misunderstood.

"It was Kate," he said. "She couldn't stop having affairs, and I couldn't stand it anymore."

Maria turned her head. "Your wife cheated on you?"

As if he were startled, he smiled. "Thanks for looking as if you can't believe it. She cheated with a vengeance."

"No one ever said a word. Not to Leila." She sat again. "Not to me."

"I'm a decent guy. I've never set a foot wrong—although maybe that was because of Leila. Kate had been with other men since before Leila was born. It was like a compulsion, but how could I explain that to Leila?"

"You couldn't." She went to him, sensing years of control, nights and days full of disappointment and wondering why he wasn't enough. "It wasn't you," she said.

He shoved his chair back. "I don't want to discuss this with you."

She knelt beside his chair. "You aren't ever going to be in my care," she said. "I couldn't be your therapist now if I wanted to be. And I don't, but I can tell you, your ex-wife has a problem, and you aren't it."

"I don't doubt myself because Kate couldn't make do with me."

"Jake." Maria took his face between her hands and made him meet her eyes. "Listen to me, and believe. I want you so much I can't think of anything except how good your hands would feel on me. I dream about you."

His smile was more delicious than any dinner anyone had ever made. He touched her face, his fingertips gentle, trembling.

"You're a kind woman."

"You're nuts." She had to convince him he didn't have to separate himself from life because he hadn't been able to singlehandedly repair his broken marriage. "You don't have to pretend to anyone else, ever, that you don't care." She reached for his hand.

His composure fled. He looked naked. Maria leaned into him, seeking his mouth and the heat that made his self-imposed detachment a thing of the past.

He groaned, and pulled her to him. It was not so much a kiss as a meeting of souls, a joining of bodies frustrated only by the clothing and the space that barely remained between them. He put his forehead against hers and undid the top buttons of her shirt.

She would never be able to treat Leila again. As much as Maria regretted failing the girl, that bridge had burned. Yet she still wasn't sure Jake trusted her.

He kissed her, slowly, thoroughly, spinning her senses almost out of control. He lifted his fingers to the next button on her shirt. She took a deep breath.

He pressed his lips to her breasts, swelling over the top of her bra.

All rational thought fled.

Her nipples ached as he opened his mouth and she felt his hunger. She breathed in the scent of him, rubbing her cheek against his hair. Without thinking, she slid to the floor, pulling him with her, still kissing him, tugging the hem of his T-shirt out of his jeans.

She slid her hands across his stomach, sighing at the scratch of sparse male hair and hot skin against her palms, breathing in as he inhaled, too. His mouth covered her nipple through her bra, and she closed her eyes as sensation raced through her body.

But then she reached the button on his jeans, and common sense screamed back into her head. She froze.

"Please," Jake said against her breast.

She managed a groan. Pleasure and a "no" wrenched from every aching sinew. This was wrong, and she couldn't tell herself that it wasn't. No matter how much she wanted to.

"Jake. Jake, I—" She staggered to her feet. "I'll do the dishes. Are you still hungry?"

"Are you out of your mind?" He sat back on

his heels. His hair was ruffled, and his heavy-lidded, startled eyes weakened her.

While he stayed where he was, she grabbed at plates, cutlery, anything except Jake. In the kitchen, she put the dishes on the counter and gripped the cool granite to keep from falling.

"Maria?"

The way he said her name was as potent as a kiss. She'd never wanted any man as badly. At last she understood why her mother and sister had made so many bad decisions.

"Maria?"

"Stay over there."

"I don't understand."

"I'm not trying to be a tease." Maria focused on the essential question between them. "I don't know if you believe me about Griff."

"What I think doesn't matter."

"It does to me." She turned away from him, back to the dishes. "And it should to you, before you sleep with me."

Silence stretched between them, filled only with the sound of Maria washing the dishes.

"That trial just won't end for us, will it?" he asked.

"Griff is free. Whatever he's done, he's free and clear."

"You're not."

She shook her head. "I don't mind it with most people, except when I think I might lose my home and starve to death." She glanced at him. "But I feel bad when I know you want sex, but you don't trust me. Though at least you don't lie about it."

"It's not just sex, Maria."

"You should go."

"Things are confused between us."

"You should still go."

SOMETIME AFTER DARK, Maria woke on the couch to find her living room glowing with twinkling colors. She hauled herself to a sitting position, flinging hair out of her eyes. What on earth?

She staggered to the windows. She tried twice before she pulled the right cord on the blinds and managed to open them all the way. The movement must have startled Jake, who looked up from furtively opening his car door.

Over every shrub, he'd strung lights. Small, starlike bits of color twinkled from all over her yard. Maria smiled.

She ran to the door to find Jake still waiting, wariness on his face. "Thanks," she said.

He nodded toward her neighbors' yards, all lights and Santas. "You needed something."

"They're beautiful." She went as far as the

bottom porch step in her turkey-stamped socks. "But you didn't have to say you were sorry."

He crossed to her. "I am sorry you misunderstand me."

"I don't, though, Jake. You made my house look happy, but you still can't say you believe me."

"I believe in you. Everyone makes mistakes."

"I didn't." She backed up a step.

Jake caught a handful of her shirt and pulled her down to kiss her in front of everyone and their puffy snowmen. "I did, and I've hurt you, but now I have to find the truth about Griff Butler. I've asked Tom Drake for the case files."

CHAPTER TEN

MONDAY MORNING, Jake called Tom Drake's office and gave the staff hell for dragging their feet about getting him Griff Butler's case files.

On Monday afternoon, Tom finally brought the files to Jake's office. Personally.

He set the stack on Jake's desk. "It's a closed case, sir." He dropped his hand on the top folder and the whole shebang threatened to topple.

"I'm sorry, Tom." But not that sorry. "I didn't realize there was so much, or I'd have sent a courier."

"We're not your personal clerks anyway, Jake."

"I get that, but I've been concerned about what happened at the trial."

"If Butler sang out his confession on the courthouse steps, we couldn't do anything now," Tom said. "I prefer to depend on the jury. The system works pretty well."

"You now think he's innocent?"

"I think I can't do anything if he's not."

"And his aunt and uncle? Their children?"

"Nothing I can do. Griff hired the more creative lawyer." Tom went to the door. "And face it, Jake. You'd be the last guy to support preemptive arrests."

"But I wouldn't mind a little creative help from your office." He sat at his desk. "Yeah, I know. Sorry about ranting now, and on the phone this morning."

"Don't worry. Kay loves having her ass chewed before coffee."

Jake pulled the chair forward. "If you'd answer your own phone or return a message, Kay would still be in possession of her ass." Maybe his own perspective was shot. "I'll call back and apologize."

"Thanks."

"How can this case be closed if the boy didn't do it?"

"That's what the jury said. At the department, we're still happy with our solution. I can't waste time on a murder that will never be solved now. Because I solved it, then your little friend had her buddy write a diary."

"My little friend?"

Tom straightened the flag that flanked the left side of Jake's door. "If you're going to string Christmas lights as a charity act, get some help. If you're hot for the shrink, try to be a little more careful until all this blows over. People in town are angry with her."

"They wouldn't be if they knew she wasn't guilty. But you've said you don't care if her story or Griff's is true."

"We determined the truth. You feel free to meddle with a closed case and try to cast aspersions on our detectives, though."

"Cut the crap, Tom."

The sheriff straightened. "Sir?"

"I don't want to make anyone look bad, but someone has called in the state's Psychology Review Board—was that you?" An impulse he couldn't control made him want to know for sure who'd turned Maria's life upside down.

"I was stunned to hear Buck brag about doing it. I thought you would have."

Jake stared at the other man for a moment before he shoved his chair back and went to the window. Below, the citizens of Honesty milled about their business. Leila wasn't the only one who thought him unfeeling. He'd never cared before. He'd done his job and done it right. He'd seen himself as a fair man who did the right thing.

"Jake, you think trying to prove we screwed up will help that woman?"

Jake gave that question the contempt it deserved. "Did Maria Keaton hurt this boy?"

The change of subject didn't make Tom any happier. "God alone knows. The diary makes you think, and nothing anyone does surprises me anymore."

"What did the diary make you think?"

Tom shrugged for an answer. "I believe he confessed to her. Doesn't mean she didn't sleep with him, but I think she was telling the truth when she testified that he told her he killed his parents."

"And you believe he killed them?"

"He had their blood on his clothing. Mud from his shoes was on his mother's sleeve. We found his father's hair on the leg of Griff's jeans."

Jake repeated Buck's argument. "They died in their home. If he found them, all of that evidence makes sense."

"Or he didn't bother to clean himself up before he called nine-one-one."

For once Jake didn't want to be any devil's advocate. "Thanks for the files, Tom. I am sorry about upsetting your assistant."

"She'll forgive you. By the way, since the case is closed, Griff was able to recover his stuff from evidence, including the journal." Tom waited at the door. "And I don't like to get in a man's personal business, but if this is about that doctor, you don't need to go public. Don't make my department look bad so you can feel good about her."

Would he do that? Destroy confidence in the police department to clear his conscience about being with a woman? "If you hear anything more about this case, you'll let me know?" He couldn't tell Tom whether his interest was in justice or in clearing Maria.

AFTER EACH MORNING'S paper route, Maria returned to her house, gazing warily at the newly draped decorations. She was so poor she wouldn't be offering anyone a commercial Christmas this year. Inside, she turned her back on her unpaid bills and took a nap. It was the only time she slept well, because she was too tired to think.

Days slipped by, bringing Christmas closer. Maria usually loved the celebration of family and hope, but this year she was afraid. She felt cut asunder, and she missed her mother. She longed to hear her sister's uninhibited laughter, but she was used to being the strong one, the reliable Keaton. She couldn't face them until she felt good about herself again.

In unguarded moments, she imagined turning to Jake, but she'd sent him firmly away, so she had only her fear of losing everything to keep her company.

As an antidote to her dark mood, she left her debit and credit cards with her checkbook in the desk drawer at home and joined the crowd siphoning into the Sugarplum and Snowflake forest in the heart of Old Honesty, where Santa held court. As soon as she arrived, though, she realized she'd made a mistake. Having already spent every penny she could afford on gifts this year, she walked around like a shooting victim, testing the pain in her wound.

She couldn't find comfort. Each colorful light seemed to mock her. Laughter burrowed under her skin as people looked away from her. She might never belong again.

Her frustration grew. Bad enough to be unemployable, but now she felt as guilty as if she had done something wrong. It was a relief when she got so fed up with averted faces and her lack of Christmas spirit that she found some healthy resentment. She didn't have to quit or give in or act guilty. She refused to hide or stop looking for work.

So she applied for a position as Santa's elf. She approached Old Honesty's business manager first, but he referred her to Santa, who ran his own show. She took her application to jolly old Saint Nick in a corner of his peppermint-studded house, but Santa shook his pink cheeks at her.

"Are you kidding?" He pulled down his beard. "I'm Marvin Henry. I live about three houses from Griff Butler's old place. That kid has problems, but I seriously doubt he killed his parents. And even if he did, Buck has me wondering whether your actions didn't make Griff do it."

"I went two years without prompting anyone to murder, but suddenly I got the urge to flex my megalomaniacal muscles?"

"Miss, I don't need an elf who's looking for her next victim. These kids come up here to tell me their dreams."

Her mouth literally dropped open. But not for long. "I would never hurt a child. My whole life has been based on helping people, and yet I'd go after the most vulnerable? Never. Buck threw a disgusting stereotype at the jury. These days people have to believe that authority figures hurt others in their care. Like a sick Santa in a small-town shop. But a wise neighbor extends the kindness of looking for proof from an otherwise blameless woman. Something not even St. Nick can do in this town."

Marvin actually blinked at her. "I guess that's your side of the story."

"The truth."

He reached into his pockets. "Maybe I'd want someone to question whether I was guilty in similar circumstances."

"That's all I'm asking."

"I still can't hire you." He actually looked troubled as he pulled a stick of peppermint from his red, fur-lined pocket. "May I offer you a candy cane?"

"I can't afford a dentist. Better lay off the sugar."

He nodded with a shaky smile, and she went away pulling at her collar as if she were catching her breath after a brawl.

She'd been turned down by almost everyone in Honesty who had a delivery schedule, a cash register, trash to haul, laundry to wash, papers to type or phones to answer. But no one until Santa had reduced her to reckless anger.

Her own four walls, soon to belong to the bank, had begun to drive her a little insane with their intimations of failure. She fled to the library with the newspaper and reworked her résumé on her laptop. She'd already canceled her Internet service at home, but using the library's public terminals she looked up an updated local business listing that gave her leads she hadn't been able to find in the phone book.

She'd keep passing out résumés until they showed up on light poles like missing puppy posters.

Halfway down the long aisle to "her" carrel, she found Jake, leaning over a back issue of the paper. He straightened when he saw her, and his eyes went all watchful and self-protective. She couldn't tell if he was remembering the way they'd kissed each other, or if he feared she might attack him in the way of all perved-out psychologists. But maybe that last was unfair.

She hadn't heard a word from him since Thanksgiving.

If she ever got her license cleared, she'd remember how she felt at this moment before she blithely told a client that healing only came when he learned to let go of a grudge.

"How are you?" Jake asked.

"Good. Not busy enough." Quite an understatement, but she hoped to sound jaunty. She put one hand to the shoulder strap of her laptop case. "And you?"

He crossed his arms over the paper so that his elbows and upper body covered most of the print. Maybe she was desperate for someone to analyze, but Jake looked as if he was trying to hide something.

"Research," he said.

She tried hard not to look, but in the end she saw half of Griff's solemn face staring back at her above Jake's sleeve.

"Holy— What are you doing?" She set her laptop on the headlines, glancing furtively at the patrons around them. "I asked you to leave it alone."

"I want to know about the case. I wasn't allowed to research the news reports before."

"But now you can, to better judge if I'm a liar?" she asked.

One of the librarians rose from her chair at the information desk. Maria's face grew as hot as a frying pan. "Your snooping will only make it worse. I couldn't convince the jury, and no one else wants to believe me now. Even if I could prove Griff did what he said he did, he's free because of double jeopardy."

"I'm not doing this for Griff. Obviously, I'm thinking of you."

Her knees went weak—but not with ever-loving passion. "This thing between us is crazy," she said. "I don't want to give people anything else to hold against me."

A frown creased his forehead. How had Leila

ever misunderstood her father? His feelings were right out there for anyone to see.

"So you've already heard talk about us?" she asked.

"What is it with you? I sit on a bench all day—for years—and no one ever knows what I'm thinking. Now you can read my mind."

She gave him her best "come on" look.

He sat up, obviously deciding there was no point in hiding the paper now. "Yeah, I've heard some stuff."

"So why won't you listen to me? You don't know best. Everyone will think I only abandoned my sick interest in Griff to chase a man who could get me my job back."

His mouth went thin. "You wouldn't do that, would you?"

"Nice," she said. "You'll never learn to believe me." But maybe she could look at it another way. Maybe he didn't think she could be interested in him for anything except ulterior motives. Something had to be behind his inability to trust anyone's emotions.

"I'm trying to believe everything you've said. But these stories are full of Griff's innocence. Put everything he said together with the journal, and I have to wonder at least what was in his head."

"The journal?" Her stomach slapped at her feet. "You have that?"

"What if I do?"

Lying wasn't his best skill. "Don't test me, Jake. I see what you're trying to make me say."

"So say it."

That husky tone in his voice usually tempted her. But, this time, anger trumped desire.

"I have said it, over and over, and you choose not to believe."

"I don't have the journal."

"You really were testing me."

As she was on her way anywhere but near him, he rose and caught her arm. "I'm out of my depth. I don't know what to think, and I can't manage to hide anything from you."

"You're not supposed to hide things from people who—"

The librarian started their way this time. Thank God. She'd saved Maria from claiming she mattered to Jake.

He eased her into the chair across from his and waved off the poor woman trying to keep the peace.

"The journal was part of Griff's personal effects, but if you think about it, a careful read might have given us something to refute his claims."

"Don't you see that reading it would have meant Griff was partially right? I'd have been almost the worst kind of therapist."

"But not interested in seducing a client," Jake said as if reminding her.

"Never that," she said, uncertain whether to laugh with relief or simply pretend she didn't consider his acceptance a gift.

Jake sighed. "I have the case files and the public record and I'm playing detective. Maybe I can find something all the other investigators missed."

What more powerful way was there to admit she mattered to him? In turn, she didn't want him to compromise his own reputation. "You don't have to do that for me."

"I'm doing it for me, because I've hurt you and I wish I hadn't."

"You didn't make that call, Jake, and wishing you had only hurts my feelings."

"Maybe that's what bothers me most."

Across the table, the attraction she couldn't control swirled between them. She wished the room would empty. "It doesn't change anything. I was your daughter's therapist. I pretty much single-handedly set a killer free, and I'm a scourge in your neighborhood."

"You couldn't prove you're innocent," he

said, reaching across the table to rest the tips of his fingers against hers. "Maybe I can."

She felt as if she couldn't breathe. She remembered his dark hair beneath her chin as he'd made her breasts ache. She felt a familiar emptiness that was growing too painful to bear.

"You and I are both doing things we've never done before. It can't be right." She found her feet.

"Why not consider that we both need to try something different to make our lives right?" Jake asked.

Maria shook her head. The familiar—and the safe—comforted her. "Let the board do its investigation, but leave everything—and everyone—else alone. Don't jeopardize your place in this town."

She marched to a table close to an electrical socket, but far, far from Judge Jake Sloane.

MARIA WAS CONCENTRATING on not looking at Jake when her phone vibrated in her jeans pocket. She jumped up and hurried across the library, not daring to miss a call that might mean a job interview.

Outside, in the vestibule, she got a shock when she looked at the caller's name. Gail Keaton. Maria hit the talk button. "Mother?"

"When are you going to fix all this, Maria?

You were always my good girl. The one of us who knew what to do next. I saw another article in the paper today. It was disgusting." She rattled the offending newspaper. "Oh, this is last week's, but they seem to assume you—"

Another shock. Maria hadn't realized her mother had ever noticed. She sighed, with the weariness that was rapidly becoming her constant companion. "I didn't—"

"Sleep with a kid? Why would you do that? Even I—"

Sometimes *Even I* started a confession that made Maria want to set her own ears on fire. "I didn't do it, Mother," she cut in. "He lied. I've already told you that."

"That jury believed him. Juries are smart."

"But I'm not a liar. I don't care who believed him. I didn't do it, and I'm trying not to mind that my mother thinks I did."

"I don't, necessarily. I just wonder if you'd want to be honest with me. Why didn't you tell me when all this first started?"

"I didn't think you'd be interested. Most of our communication comes from…" She stopped.

"The checks you send me? I appreciate the help. You know I do, but, obviously, I want to hear if you're having an affair with a younger man."

"Mother, sleeping with a sixteen-year-old

boy is abuse, not an affair, and you don't have to assume that paper is telling the truth and I'm lying."

"Don't get mad at me. People do it all the time these days, and I called because I'm worried about you."

"Okay." She took a deep breath and let it go. Grudges against her mother never ended well for either of them. "I'm glad you called, because I needed to let you know I might have to stop sending you help, Mom. I'm suspended from working."

"I'm worried about you," her mother repeated. "I didn't call about the money, although that does give me pause. You know I don't have a retirement fund."

"I'll do what I can."

"Your sister's been helping me out, too. Clowns do a surprisingly good business."

Maria shuddered. Clowns scared the crap out of her. How kids didn't run screaming when Bryony showed up in all her big-shoed, green-haired, maniacally smiling glory was beyond anything Maria would ever understand.

"You should maybe ask Bryony for help, Maria. She could show you how to do the makeup. Give you a few of her gigs."

It was as if her mother had never made her

acquaintance. "That's certainly an idea, but I need to go. I left my laptop open in the library when I came outside to answer your call."

"Oh, dear. Someone will steal that. You go back now, but let me know what's going on with you."

"Don't worry."

"If I were you, I'd get that diary back before it ends up in a paper or online somewhere."

Maria turned slowly toward the white French doors that separated her from the library's main collection room. And the comfort of being near Jake.

She just had to pray that her mother, Buck Collier and Griff Butler didn't think alike.

"I didn't do anything. Whatever the kid wrote is fiction." But what if Jake thought it was the only place he could find the truth? What if he pressured Griff's aunt and uncle for a look at that journal? They'd let him see it because he had power.

He could speak out for their nephew against a prowling cougar.

She couldn't bear the thought of Jake reading lies the jury had believed.

"Maria, did you hear me? Get that thing back before someone sells it to a tabloid and you find yourself on one of those fair and balanced inquisitions."

"I love you, Mom. I have to go."

"You're not listening to me." Gail sighed. "Well, I hope that means you aren't worrying too much. I'm sure you'll get your work back soon."

Her mother might have bad taste and not nearly enough respect for herself when it came to men, but she maintained a consistently sunny attitude that she was happy to share. Looking at the world with a little less optimism and a touch more acuity might have kept her out of gallons of her own hot water over the years.

But for today, Maria latched on to her mother's point of view.

"Thanks for the advice, Mom. I'll call you."

She hit the off button and slid her phone back into her pocket, trying to catch her breath. The idea of the diary showing up in the media made her feel ill. But the thought of Jake hunched over that scratched-up, worn-out, thick-with-writing notebook made her nearly crazy with panic. She cared about him, and she wanted his good opinion. She'd hate for him to believe the ugly things Griff Butler must have written.

Maria pushed into the collection room. Jake hadn't moved. He looked up as if he sensed her coming. Without taking her customary moment to consider repercussions, she slid into the chair next to Jake's, not sure what she was going to say.

The librarian was up again. Maria ignored

her. No one and no rules mattered. She didn't even care that she was about to make herself look totally guilty.

"Jake," she said, "please don't try to get that diary from Griff's aunt and uncle."

He stared at her, his breath warm on her mouth, his eyes sad and watchful enough to make her feel lost. At last, he lifted his hand and nudged her bangs out of her eyes.

"Are you all right? What's wrong?"

She caught his hand, then pushed it away from her, because the thing she wanted most was to pull him close and confess that she was afraid and desperate enough to risk even the self-respect that had been her most valuable trait. "Don't read that thing."

"I won't," he said, and if they'd been anywhere except a library, she'd have thrown him onto his back and kissed him senseless. "If it matters so much to you."

She didn't know how to thank him. She felt too vulnerable to speak. He might not know she'd just admitted that clearing her name meant less than keeping him from even imagining Griff's ugly fantasies might be true. With her throat as tight as a closed fist, she nodded and hurried to her own table.

CHAPTER ELEVEN

THAT WAS A ROUGH NIGHT. She had no idea if Jake was refusing to read the diary because he believed it was a lie, or because he hated the fact that Griff had written about her that way. She should have asked.

She should have done something. Any action might have saved her a night of tossing in her bed, wishing she could learn how to guard her dignity from the staid citizens of Honesty, who'd circled their small-town wagons.

In the morning, she dressed and steeled herself for another smack-down from a possible employer. Yesterday, walking home from the library after the stores had closed, she'd spotted a Help Wanted sign in the pharmacy, seeking a cashier.

Maria hadn't bothered to call first. This job, she had a better shot at. Even without an M.D., she had some understanding of pharmacology.

And she saw no reason to give potential employers the chance to turn her down over the phone. Let them do it to her face.

She sat on a blue chair opposite the counter while the pharmacist went to the back to read her application and résumé. It was a slow process as customers came and went. Some, she knew. No one said hello.

Mr. Baxter, a former client, darted into the shelter of the store's crowded aisles the second he saw her. Despite the situation, she smiled at his efforts to break all speed records. Was he running from the horror of talking to her, or had he suffered a setback with his kleptomania?

She'd begun to assume the pharmacist was also avoiding her until he finally came to the counter. "Dr. Keaton?"

"Maria," she said.

"I'm Robert Collins." He held her application in both hands. "Why don't you come on back? You deserve the truth."

That sounded bad, but she didn't know how to walk away. She had to stop expecting the worst.

The man led her to his office and offered her a chair. Maria sat, placing her feet neatly side by side on the floor. Funny how a scandal made you überaware of every little nuance.

"I'm glad to meet you, Maria." Mr. Collins

took off his glasses and placed them just as precisely on his blotter. "But I think you know this will be a fruitless visit. You must realize by now that no one in this town will hire you."

She was becoming an expert on pretending the blows glanced off. "I don't know that." He didn't smile. She fended him off with a lame joke. "I might get a persecution complex."

He shook his head, a sage in a lab coat. "I'm more familiar with pharmacology than Freud, but I believe it's only a complex when you just think everyone's out to get you."

"I don't understand you, Mr. Collins. You speak like an honorable man. You asked me back to your office instead of throwing me out or making up something like 'the position's been filled.' Why do you assume I'm guilty when I haven't even been on trial?"

"I'm not so honorable. I tried to wait you out." His skin turned pink beneath and around his thick mustache. "But you wouldn't leave."

"No."

"So I'm going to explain, and I'll repeat myself because I'd like to save you from future embarrassment. No one in this town will ever hire you."

"Mr. Herbert at the department store said the same thing."

"Why do you keep trying?"

"Because Honesty has been my home for two years, and I want to stay. I did nothing wrong, and I need to work. I cannot sit around and do nothing while people I don't know decide my future." She stood. "And I thought that maybe since you're providing a service that deals with science and health, I'd stand a better chance with you. I took classes in pharmacology, and I've kept up my knowledge."

"It doesn't matter, Maria. You're tied up in a scandal with a boy from one of Honesty's oldest families. I can't afford to discourage people from coming to my window. I have regulars who'd go all the way to D.C. to teach me a lesson if I hired you. I've even heard some suggest you drugged Griff."

"What?"

"You might have hurt that boy so much you drove him to kill his parents. How does anyone here know?"

"But he was acquitted."

"I've heard many testimonials about you before now, but I don't think you understand the psyche of a five-generation Honesty citizen. No one on that jury wanted to blame their own small-town aristocracy. Even if they thought Griff was guilty, they'd acquit him if they could blame his crime on something you did to him."

"I tried to help Griff. I'm not even sure I would have turned him in to the police if the law didn't require it."

"Forgive me for being salacious, but a lot of people here believe you tried to *help* him. They just don't know when sex became part of a boy's therapy."

Maria stood, tucked her purse beneath her elbow and wished the little store had a public shower. "You didn't have to bring me back here to tell me what you thought of me." Before he could answer, "We Wish You a Merry Christmas" came jingling out of the PA system. Maria shook her head at the speaker above his desk. "That's a laugh."

"Hearts still beat around here. Just not for you," he said. "I'm not trying to be cruel, and I don't share my neighbors' bad opinion. I don't even know you, except for what I've heard people say." He shrugged. "I feel bad for you because I've also heard other business owners talking about your job interviews. You need to stay out of sight and let this blow over. If Griff Butler's guilty, he'll show some other sign, and people will realize they've misjudged you."

She stared at him. It was a funny way to help. "Thanks," Maria said doggedly as she turned and walked toward his office door. "I won't make this mistake anymore." She paused on the threshold and looked back. "You do realize if Griff Butler betrays himself, it might result in someone else dying?"

"I'm well aware. I don't know how many of my friends are."

Sighing with frustration, Maria turned, only to find Jake waiting at the counter, clearly trying not to listen. Had she swallowed some kind of magnet that dragged him to the site of her every humiliation?

"Hello." She tried hard not to stare into his eyes, but when she was hurt, she wanted to go to him. It was ridiculous. He was not her friend. They had some crazy guilt-and-loneliness thing going on that made them want to have sex. Her awareness of him was so overpowering that she almost stumbled as she walked past him through an open space in the counter.

"Maria, are you all right?"

"Jake? How can I help you?" Mr. Collins asked behind her.

Jake seemed reluctant to break eye contact with her as he turned to the waiting pharmacist. Maria breathed out. How desperate had she become? She overanalyzed every move he made, each glance he spared her. She couldn't afford to turn into a Keaton woman, who started looking for a man—any man—at the first sign of trouble.

The thought made her uncomfortable, both for its cruelty to her semireformed mother and sister, and for its possible truth about her.

She turned away from Jake.

"I need to pick up a prescription for my aunt," he said to the druggist.

"Ah. Helen's digitalis. I have it right back here. I'll go over the cautions with you, and you remind her of them. She'll tell you she already knows how she's supposed to take her medication, but you make her listen. Every time I cover the side effects with her, she acts as if she's never heard of them. We wouldn't want her to forget."

Maria ducked behind the first aisle and stood with her back to the shelves, trying to calm her racing heart. She hadn't been this rattled since the first time her mother had sent her and her sister outside while an "uncle" visited.

Jake and Mr. Collins spoke to each other like friends who cared. They'd lived in Honesty all their lives. Long enough to earn unconditional trust.

She didn't notice Jake and the other man had stopped talking until Jake showed up, obviously searching for her.

Maria curled her hands into fists. She should go. His compassion was an intimate, tangible thing that wrapped her in its arms before he even came near her.

"What is happening to you?" he asked.

"Nothing. I'm fine."

"Liar." But he wrapped the ugly word in husky concern as he pulled her close.

"This is a public place." Her tongue felt thick. She could hardly put the words together.

He shook his head as his mouth hovered over hers. "I don't care. I need—"

So did she. She locked her arms behind his neck, trying to get closer, her only urgent longing to feel she belonged to someone.

And Jake kissed her as if he belonged to her. His mouth opened hers. He tasted of morning coffee. His hands slid inside her coat, clenching in the small of her back to pull her into him.

She didn't care about the vague memory of security cameras that flitted through her mind, or the far-off tinkle of a bell over an opening door. Even the new sound of voices didn't bother her.

Wanting to be in Jake's arms, wanting him to make her forget everything that had gone so wrong, frightened her more than any disembodied threat or disgusted but self-righteous store owner.

"I need you, too," she said, finding sweet consolation in the hunger on Jake's drawn face. "But I can't have you if I don't know why I need you."

"That's up to me, too, isn't it?"

"I wish it were."

She pulled away from him, her hands sliding over his cheeks as she tried to imprint the texture of his skin on her memory.

"Maybe, after I fix all my problems—" she began, but couldn't finish. She hurried to the front of the store. As she turned toward the doors, she saw a mirror that reflected all the aisles. Her skin burned as she laughed, embarrassment mixed with skin-raking desire.

THE STORE'S BELL PEALED AGAIN as Maria darted out the front. Jake stayed where he was, damn near unable to walk.

She kept telling him to stop meddling, and God knows he'd lived his entire life taking a neutral position in battles like the one she was fighting. But Maria seemed to think she could cope completely on her own. She imagined her feelings were the only ones involved.

He hadn't trusted his feelings for a woman in who knows how long?

Yeah, there'd been brief relationships. But what man even knew what the word *relation-*

ship meant? There'd been nights with eager women who'd made him forget Kate had never been content to settle for only him.

Women he'd chosen in part because he believed in their discretion in a small town. Leila's reaction to her father sleeping with anyone had never been far from his mind, despite the divorce. Maybe, deep down, he'd realized she hadn't adjusted to it.

Now he was willing to risk everything for a few moments with Maria.

He had to understand.

He went to the front of the store, too, tucking his aunt's medication into the pocket of his overcoat. Helen and her demon dog herd lived a few doors down from Maria.

"Jake?"

He turned back. Robert Collins was flapping after him, his glasses glinting, his white coat flying, his face determined.

MARIA PAUSED in putting her icicle decorations on last year's nails. One of them had worked far enough out to lean at an angle. Balancing on the railing, she leaned down for her hammer, but tilted mid-reach and managed to shove it into the shrubbery that lined her porch.

Above her swearing, she heard footsteps crunching up the icy walk. She almost fell as Jake stepped onto the porch. After taking off his shoe, he climbed onto the railings beside her and used the heel to hammer in the nail.

"There's a hammer down there."

Pristine in his black overcoat and suit, he glanced into the yard. "I'm not climbing in the evergreens."

"You make me conspicuous every time you beat on my door."

"I didn't get that far yet."

If she were wise, he wouldn't. "What are you doing here again?"

He jumped down, slipped on his shoe then reached up for her. Without thinking, she let him take her waist and covered his hands with hers. As he eased her to safety, she slid down his body and felt anything but safe.

"I'm not going away," he said, reading her mind.

Would it be worse to fight or risk giving in to wanting him? He wasn't about to back down.

"You'd better come in." She twisted away from him and he followed her into the house. "It was a mistake in the store," she said. "What we did." The last came out in a whisper.

"No."

"Yes, Jake."

"We can't help what we feel."

"I'm trained to believe we can choose how to behave," she said, though aching for him made her question every decision she'd ever made. Maybe she hadn't ever wanted anything enough before.

Jake closed the front door and peeled off his coat. He threw it over the back of her sofa. "Robert Collins came after me in the store. He tried to explain why he'd spoken up."

"Oh my God," she said, taking off her own coat and hanging it in the closet. "It's not bad enough we made out in front of a security mirror. You gossiped with the pharmacist."

"I may have suggested he do several things most men couldn't manage on their own, but I didn't chat with him about you. Then I offered to break him in several pieces so as to make my other suggestions more manageable." His rueful smile made Maria smile, too.

"I thought you were talking about your aunt's medication."

"It was after you left. At first he wanted to leave bad enough alone, but he thought I might be a friend of yours."

"Everyone knows you are. We haven't been particularly discreet." The gossips probably thought they understood her relationship with Jake perfectly. It was ironic, really, because she didn't understand it at all. She turned toward the kitchen. "Do you want something warm to drink?"

"No." He took her hand and pulled her close. "I want to hold you." He rested his forehead against hers, and she closed her eyes, knowing she should send him away.

But temptation was too strong, and she leaned into him, hungry for even another second in his arms. A second she would hoard in her memory. When life was normal again and Mr. I-Must-Wreak-Justice got over his guilt, there would be no more moments like this. Only their mutual need made them alike.

"Maria?"

She opened her eyes. He bent his head. His mouth brushed hers. "I'd give anything to make everyone see what I do when I look at you."

Maria lifted her head. "What do you see? Who do you see?"

"A woman I want." He smiled, his mouth sensual and generous, stirring the most basic need deep inside her. "Maybe I'm looking at the woman for me."

"There speaks guilt." She pretended her heart wasn't battering at the walls of her chest.

"I don't know what to say." He took her mouth, quick and hard and hot. "We work best together when we stop talking." He grasped both sides of her collar. "Can we lock this door?"

"No one will come in."

"I want to be alone with you."

"Alone?"

He slid both hands around her shoulders and covered her mouth again, gently this time, but when he deepened the kiss and she felt her control spiraling away, she flattened her palms against his chest. His hands released her, but his savage, yearning gaze held on.

Consequences. She'd never made a move without considering them.

"Think about this, Jake. Are you a man who can make love and walk away?"

"I have," he said.

It hit her like a punch in the stomach. "I never expected you to say that."

"You look scared." Jake twisted his mouth. Simple discomfort? Defiance? The will to bludgeon her with the truth? "You're analyzing me? Now?"

She blushed. He reached for her collar. His hands moved to the buttons on her blouse.

"I'm not like any woman you've walked away from." She covered his fingers. "But I'm not right for you. Not even on a normal day, when you aren't riddled with guilt."

"Shut up, Maria." He bent his head. His lips grazed her throat. He opened his lips against her skin, and she fell against his heat, his taunting, teasing, beautiful mouth.

Her top several buttons were open.

"You move fast."

"I'm like magic." He put his hand to the knot on his tie, and the silk soon dropped to the floor beside them. He brought her trembling hands to the buttons on his black shirt. "You work magic, too."

"I'm afraid."

"I know how tough you are." Clearly, he meant she was not. "But I won't hurt you."

"We're bound to hurt each other."

"What do you mean?"

"You have to let this thing with Griff go. You'll drag yourself into trouble when folks realize you feel more for the town harlot than you should."

"I asked you to stop talking," he said, but somehow the words meant, *Undo my shirt. Touch me.*

He unfastened his own buttons. His shirt fell open, revealing the sparse, dark hair on his chest. She stared at his pulse, throbbing like crazy. Without thinking, she lifted her hands and pressed her fingertips to his skin.

A sound seeped from her mouth, need and relief all at once, as his muscles jumped beneath her palms. "Jake." She pressed her face to his breastbone, breathing him in, tasting him with her lips and the tip of her tongue.

"Don't look away from me." He tilted her head up, kissing her, holding her gaze as he explored her mouth, her desire, as she ripped the tail of his shirt out of his pants, shoved his jacket off his shoulders.

Her own shirt disappeared. She kicked off her shoes. All the while, Jake was kissing her, following the curve of her throat with his hands and his mouth, sighing as he cupped her breasts in the lacy, see-through bra, then closed his teeth lightly over her skin and the lace, driving her nearly out of her mind.

She'd never thrown caution to any wind. She'd clung to it like the last rope on a hot-air balloon trying to take off without her.

But when Jake reached for his belt, her hands were there before him. They both groaned as his trousers dropped. The backs of her fingers ran across his corded muscles, tensed with the same eagerness that made her shake in his arms.

Her jeans were harder to dispense with, but

Jake pushed them down her thighs, and she finally kicked them away from her feet. Jake wrapped his arms around her waist and lifted her in his arms, kissing the hollow of her throat, the curve of her neck, roaming her body at will. He couldn't reach all the places she needed him at once, but he drugged her with his effort. She felt the wall at her back suddenly, and the savage strength of wanting made her shy.

When she tried to look down, taking cover in the curtain of her hair, Jake whispered, "No," and nudged her with his chin. He reached down and lifted her legs around his waist, his hands wandering restlessly, whipping urgent need with every movement. She arched against him, and he slowly let her down, whispering her name. As her feet touched the cool floor, she had to have his mouth again.

While she kissed him, desperate to own some small piece of him, he lowered her to the thick rug. She curved her ankles around his calves, cozying his arousal into her center. She couldn't wait much longer.

"Please," she said. "Jake…"

He strained to push the coffee table away from them. "Do you have—" He broke off. "I don't want you to think—"

"That you assume I have condoms because of

someone else?" She couldn't remember anyone else. Ever. "They're in the bathroom. We could go to my bed."

He kissed her hard, his tongue thrusting slowly with seductive, restless strokes. "We will," he finally said, dragging his thumb around her lower lip. "Sometime. Wait here."

He pulled himself up, staggering like a man intoxicated. "Where the hell is your bathroom?"

"Down the hall. Hurry."

She slid her hands beneath her back, lifting her hips in anticipation. The man had hardly touched her and she was halfway to… Well, to many good things.

"Do that again," Jake said, and Maria twisted to see him.

"Your breasts are almost out of that scrap of lace. I want to taste you." His voice was a whisper. Shocked, needful. "I want to own you."

Own? That kind of possessiveness should have frightened her. Instead, she felt part of a secret world that only she and Jake could inhabit. They were reaching out in a way she'd never dared before.

They only had to trust each other to make it safe.

But trust—that was a big risk.

CHAPTER TWELVE

SHE SHOULD RUN. She should make him leave.

Making love wouldn't turn her into a woman who needed justice over compassion, and it wouldn't stop him from thinking he could rule the world from his dispassionate spot on the bench.

"What's the matter?" he asked. Her doubts must have shown.

"Are we really ready for this?"

"You're the one who takes chances."

"Calculated ones." She ran her hands down her thighs. She wanted him so terribly.

"You're afraid?"

"You matter to me."

"I won't hurt you," he said.

"Do you know what you're saying?"

"Not really." He stared at the door. "I can still go, but I don't want to. I don't want to hurt you. I want to keep you safe."

Maria closed her eyes. She didn't need

forever. She needed intentions and desire that matched her own. If she could ask him to be the kind of man who'd changed because he had hurt her, couldn't she take one leap of faith?

She opened her eyes. "You can't touch me from over there."

"The things you do to me." He came to her, his arousal jutting in his boxers. He ripped the packet open with his teeth. His smile wrapped her in warmth and longing.

He dropped his boxers and sheathed himself, and she groaned, watching, jealous that he was touching himself instead of letting her do it.

He knelt between her legs and reached beneath her for the catch on her bra. As he leaned down to capture a nipple, lace and all, he sucked so strongly she damn near wept with pleasure.

She ran her palms over his shoulders, loving the texture and the heat of him, asserting her claim, reveling in the ripple of his skin and his ragged voice calling her name as he moved to her other breast.

His trembling hands went down her waist. She felt vulnerable, and more feminine than she ever had before because her curves pleased him. This was the feeling that drove her, this connection that went beyond soul to soul.

"I can't get you close enough," she said.

He tugged her panties down her legs, following their progress with his mouth. His lips tortured her, sleek and moist.

He lifted himself over her and stared into her eyes. Harsh desire changed his features. He was foreign and yet achingly familiar, rubbing her with himself, begging for entry, teasing her as he backed away.

He moved in, but then out again.

"Jake." Her voice broke as she locked her hands on his hips.

"Hmm?" He thrust deeper, but not deep enough.

She breathed in, unable to control a sob.

"You can't wait?"

She shook her head. She also couldn't bear his dark gaze that saw too much of her, looked too deeply inside her. She raised herself and nuzzled his neck, tasting moisture, kissing her way to his earlobe.

It was his turn to groan. He tried to find her face, but she exacted her own revenge. She evaded his hands, opening her mouth against him, kissing another path to the flat tight nipple that contracted the second she touched him with her tongue.

Still, he held back. She lifted her hips, licking his salty skin. He surged into her, his hands going to the small of her back, holding her as he panted into her hair.

They hung together, half off the floor, straining against each other. Maria had never wanted so much. She'd never felt so bathed in joy.

He moved, and she moved with him, against him. They danced as one, and the floor might have been the softest bed. Jake pushed one hand beneath her head, chasing her mouth with his, taking her in all the ways a man could.

And she gave him all that she had left. Herself.

With a cry of startled delight, she tightened around him, laughing as he grunted and then raced to catch up with her. He pulsed inside her, and she felt powerful because she had kept him from lasting. She had pushed him, with the need he alone had awakened.

With the control that seemed to be his pride and her pleasurable frustration, he'd tried to grip the sanity he'd driven her to forsake, but his body had been unable to resist hers.

Minutes afterward, his harsh breathing drew goose bumps on her neck and shoulders. He kissed her, gently, luxuriantly, as if they had forever. He cradled her chin against him, taking her mouth over and over, as if he, too, could never get enough.

"You mentioned a bed?"

She nodded.

"As soon as I'm able to walk," he said, smiling, "we'll try that out, too."

She looped her arms around his neck, rocked their still-entwined bodies. "I'm content."

His mouth felt different. He kissed her with the knowledge of a lover, stirring her body with his need. "You aren't content yet," he said.

As they lay together, a sudden knock at the door made them freeze.

"The windows," she said. "The drapes are all open."

Jake reached over her head and dragged his shirt to them. "Put this on."

He sat up and grabbed his boxers. She yanked his shirt on and did up the buttons. Jake stood, but she took his hand.

"Whoever it was hasn't knocked again."

"I know. Who knocks once and goes away?"

"Someone who saw your car here and doesn't like me? Someone who doesn't want you to be with me?"

"You mean, Leila?"

"No," she said, horrified.

But Jake pulled on his pants. He looked sexier than ever with his belt dangling, the dark hair on his flat belly arrowing toward his open zipper.

She stood, too, unsteady on her feet. She

would never hurt Leila on purpose. Her heart broke for the girl who'd never understood her parents' breakup.

"I have to see if it was her." Jake zipped his pants and then went toward the door. She followed, but he eased her out of the way with his arm.

"Stay back," he said.

"If you're going, I am, too."

"I'm not going. I just want to see."

"What if it is someone who wants to hurt one of us? What if it's Griff? His aunt and uncle live near here, too, and no one ever found the gun."

"That little shit doesn't scare me." He opened the door and peered into the twilight.

Maria stood behind him, staring at the man who retained none of his indifference.

"It's dark outside," Jake said. "I don't see anyone."

For once, the sky was clear. Moonlight reflected off the snow, illuminating Maria's yard all the way to the street, but she saw no one, either.

"Come back." She tugged his arm, and he let her pull him away from the door. He turned to shove it shut.

Maria darted around him to lock it. Jake was already pulling the blinds.

"I'm not going anywhere," he said.

"What?"

"Someone might have heard I've picked up Griff's case files." He caught her close, and she didn't know if she was trembling simply because she was in his arms, or if she was afraid of noises going bump in the night. "I hope that bed's big enough for two."

"If we stick together."

MUCH LATER, long after most sober Honesty citizens had finished their evening meal and cleaned away its remains, sent the children to bed and sought their own rest, Maria was scrambling eggs.

"Cheese." Jake turned from the fridge, brandishing it. "How broke are you, Maria?"

Ah, the harsh light of reality. "Not quite yet. Something about my cheese makes you ask?"

"Something about your empty refrigerator. I'd kill for a cup of coffee."

"I'll make some." She kissed his cheek, but wrinkled her nose at the scratch of his beard. "You have no clean clothes to put on in the morning."

"Let's not talk about morning yet." He grabbed a knife and cutting board from the drainer and began to shave slices of cheese.

"I can't hide with you in my little haven forever," she said, glancing toward the window over the sink. She'd drawn the curtains she rarely closed. She hardly ever remembered they were there, using that window only to look over her hard-to-tame back garden. "But I'm glad you're here."

He offered her a bite of cheddar, letting his thumb linger so that she licked it.

"You're not tired, are you?" he asked with the hoarse note she already recognized.

"Yes," she admitted, "but I don't want to sleep."

After they ate, they washed dishes and then turned off the lights and returned to her room.

"Ready for a shower?" he asked.

"With you?"

He laughed, and his hands persuaded her, sliding over her body as he tugged her toward the bathroom. They made slow, wet love beneath the spray, and he carried her to bed afterward because her legs were too weak to support her. Or so she pretended.

IN THE MORNING, Jake rose first and went back to the shower. Maria debated joining him, but he had to show up in court. She slipped out of bed and stepped into his boxers, laughing softly as they slid low on her hips.

In the kitchen, she whipped up coffee and toast. She was heading down the hall to ask if he wanted something else when he came out of the bathroom in a towel.

He stopped, fresh desire darkening his eyes. "Nice outfit."

"I like them."

He tugged at the waistband. "I'm not getting them back?"

"Depends on how you ask. Do you want more eggs?"

He hugged her, pressing his mouth to the top her head. "I'll bring groceries tonight."

"Are you coming back?"

He looked down at her. She'd never liked being short, but somehow, she felt all feminine when Jake eyed her from his height. She laughed.

"That means I can?" he asked.

"You're giving me a choice?"

He kissed her cheek. "I can be trained. Come watch me dress."

"Sounds like fun." She was already calculating the time they still had before he was due at the courthouse when she remembered her own job. "Oh, no. My paper route."

She ran past Jake and scrambled into her jeans, not caring that his boxers bunched like an extra pair of pants.

"Your what?" His voice broke with a laugh.

"It's the only job I've been able to find." She

grabbed a sweatshirt and then yanked on socks. Jake was still mesmerized, waiting at the bedroom door in his towel.

"You have a paper route? You deliver papers?"

"I have to go," she said. "I'll be lucky if there are any papers left. I can't afford to be fired."

"Are you the reason I can't ever find my paper? Are you the one who's been throwing it in the neighbor's topiary?"

"You are one funny guy. I'll leave my spare key by the door." She looked him over. It would be okay. They were going too fast, but love might work like that sometimes. "Will you lock up before you leave?"

"Call me when you come back," he said. "I want to hear your voice."

She froze. His acceptance of whatever had happened between them made her wary. She didn't feel so sanguine. Satiated, but not sanguine. Forcing herself to move, she grabbed a brush and tugged it through her knotted hair. Her eyes teared—at the tangles. Only at the pain of brushing tangles out of her hair.

"Something's bothering you," Jake said.

"What's happening?" she asked.

"Do we have to know?"

"I'd like to know," she said. "Since we had

sex in front of my open windows, the neighbors probably know."

Jake was silent for several long seconds. "You're just trying to seduce me again, aren't you?"

She almost thanked him for letting her off the hook. But before she could say anything so ridiculous, she turned and caught a glimpse of herself in the mirror. Her jeans were lumpy. A fold of boxers stuck out beneath her sweatshirt. Her hair—Bryony would want a wig based on this do.

"Maria, don't analyze. We're fine. We'll figure it out, but until we do, lock your doors, okay?"

"I do lock my doors."

"I'm worried about that bang on the front one last night."

"It was just kids or a bird."

"In November? A turkey fleeing someone's holiday dinner?" He nodded. "All this talk in town might have made someone angry with you."

Maria set down her brush. "Don't even think about sticking your neck out to protect me."

"See you tonight," Jake said, his tone so solemn and unwavering she barely found strength or reason to argue.

"Okay, but please, Jake—" she touched his hand "—don't do anything else with those files. Don't interrogate anyone. Don't even talk to

Griff. I don't want more trouble. I don't want you to get in trouble on my behalf, and neither of us needs any further gossip."

With a quizzical smile, he kissed the tip of her nose. She tugged him closer and kissed him the way she already knew he liked best. When he pushed his hands beneath her sweatshirt, she wriggled out of his reach.

"This is the only way I can get your attention."

"I am listening," he said.

"Then hear me. I'm serious." She ran down the hall, grabbed the spare house key from a drawer in the kitchen and fumbled with the locks on her front door. She finally got it open only to find her sister on the front step.

"What?" Maria asked, managing nothing more intelligent.

"Mom said you might need help." Bryony lifted her hands, theatrically taking hold of the icy morning. "And I can tell already. What this town needs is a clown."

It was the slogan, on her business cards and her billing slips. It was written in hot pink on a magnetic strip that ran down the side of a black Jeep parked in Maria's driveway.

"Oh, my." Bryony stared over her shoulder, and Maria knew of only one sight in her house that could render a woman openmouthed in shock.

She turned, ready to ask Jake to put something over the towel. But he had. He just looked equally good in open-zipped pants and nothing else. He shrugged, his take-your-breath-away mouth tilting in a self-conscious grin as he zipped his pants.

"I guess you don't have to lock up now," Maria said to Jake. "Bryony, this is Jake Sloane. Jake, my sister, Bryony."

"Hello." Offering his hand, he came to the door. Bryony had the look of a Keaton woman ready to fall. Maria prayed she wouldn't.

"I came to help my sister."

"Oh," Maria said, not at her most eloquent. Bryony had "helped" her before. They'd learned they could best stay sisters and friends with distance between them.

"Maria's thinking I'll probably make things worse, but I'm glad to have the chance to prove I've changed."

"Bryony? You know you've never met this man?"

"He seems to know you well."

Maria's skin flamed. She dared not look at Jake.

"Give me a chance, Maria."

How could she take money from her sister? Or maybe her lesson for this visit was that she was supposed to give up one more guy to her gorgeous, extroverted sibling.

But she wouldn't let Jake go without hand-to-hand combat.

She leaned around her sister, kissed Jake with a hint she simply couldn't resist of "he's mine," and then ran for her car. "I'll be back in a couple of hours, Bryony. See you tonight, Jake."

CHAPTER THIRTEEN

AFTER A FRUITLESS SEARCH of Maria's porch and the shrubbery around it, Jake was late when he took his seat behind the bench and waved the jury and the gallery into theirs. Gil Daley was back at the prosecutor's table. Jake schooled himself to feel no bias because of what had happened to Maria in Gil's hands.

"Come to order," he said. This time, Gil was prosecuting a car thief named Cal Richardson who'd offended against the community and then offended again at least four times that Jake knew of. Cal claimed each of the owners had lent their vehicles to him. Wait, no—he suggested on the stand, to his own attorney's despair, that maybe they'd hired him to sell the cars.

The jury wasn't supposed to know that Cal's career in Honesty had been broken up by a stretch in the prison over in Layton, but it was an open secret. Probably half the jury knew Cal.

So they'd have to overcome their own assumptions to do the right thing and give him a fair trial. Decide this case according to the evidence, rather than knowledge of Cal's past. Jake wished the man luck. Griff's jury had judged both Maria and Griff on the basis of gossip.

Jake looked down at his laptop screen. Blank. Usually, he kept his own notes on each case. Facts, hints, legal questions he needed to research. But today he was a different man. He couldn't keep his mind on his job. He made himself a note to ask for today's transcript.

Wouldn't it have been wiser to make sure Maria was innocent before he'd made love with her? They'd crossed a line, and he prayed his daughter wouldn't suffer because he hadn't been able to rein in his emotions. He prayed Leila had contacted one of the therapists Maria had suggested.

"Your Honor," the defense said, in the tone of an attorney who expected him to rule on a motion.

"Repeat please, for the record," he said, as if the court reporter and not he had been distracted. While the attorney restated her objection, Jake glanced surreptitiously at his watch. He still had to deliver his aunt's medication.

And no matter what Maria said, he wanted a look at Griff's new home. Maybe just a drive by to see if Griff and his cousins were around. Jake rubbed his mouth. The kid wouldn't take up murder in plain sight just because he might have got away with it once in the privacy of his home.

For now, it was time Jake got his mind back on business and stopped all this "feeling." It got in the way of court.

"WHY ARE YOU SO WORRIED, Maria?" Bryony greeted her at the front door with a mug of steaming coffee. "Nobody else saw your gentleman caller, and I won't tell."

Shucking off her coat and gloves and hat, Maria avoided her sister's gaze. Growing up in their many homes, they'd both learned how to keep secrets. Her own therapist in college had said her deepest challenge would be admitting when she was afraid. And she was now.

She cared so much for Jake she was taking ridiculous chances with her reputation. She'd let him see how vulnerable her feelings for him made her. Bryony would have to be blind to miss the fact that Maria was half in love with Jake already, but Maria had to convince her sister she was still the rational, responsible Keaton.

She took the mug and flashed her best brittle smile. "I'm not afraid you'll sell pictures to the newspaper."

Bryony touched her arm. "Not so sure I won't

go after your guy, though? It's been a long time since I got a kick out of stealing other girls' boyfriends."

"Jake's not my boyfriend. Women my age do not have boyfriends."

"Normal ones who don't fear looking irresponsible," Bryony said. "You should give yourself credit. Attitude is everything, and your attitude has changed."

Maria lifted her head. "Because I'm known for seducing little boys?"

"I never believed that for a second."

"Not capable of seducing?" She took a painfully hot sip of her coffee and barely managed to swallow, choking. She held up her hand. "My God, that was a stupid thing to say."

"I push your buttons." Bryony shrugged. "I'm sorry about that." She nudged Maria toward the kitchen. "But you never understood about the boys. Or me. I knew you disapproved of me. It made me angry."

"So you thought taking any guy who was interested in me was a good idea?"

"It was good, if ugly, revenge. I never realized you'd think I was going to stay that girl for the rest of my life."

"I'm not very healthy where you and Mom are concerned."

"How could you be? We can barely spend time in the same town, and Mom still mooches off you."

Maria opened her mouth, but Bryony cut her off.

"I know. That was supposed to be your secret, but Mom asked if I could make up the difference."

"I don't mind helping her. I'm just tired of my own mess and worried that I won't be able to provide for both of us."

"So you can't be her 401k?"

Her tone mocked herself as much as their mother. Maria carried her mug to the kitchen, whose warmth reassured her. "I try not to think like that now. I have no room to judge anyone else. I just worry about Mom. And you."

"Maybe you didn't even want Jake to know about us."

"All right." She turned at the bar stools. "Cut it out. If you want to argue, say what's on your mind."

"I got the idea you were ashamed of me when you introduced us."

"You misunderstood." Maria sat at the bar and caught sight of an egg casserole and biscuits. "And you've been cooking."

"I wouldn't starve you just because you don't want me here. You're too thin."

"I want you here." Maria wasn't sure she did, but that was her problem, not Bryony's. "But I didn't expect you this morning, and I wasn't hoping to show off a—" What? A new relationship? That was too tame.

"A lover?" Bryony asked.

"Jake. He never stayed here before. I may have acted sanctimonious with you and Mom all our lives, but your opinion matters to me. Jake and I don't know each other well enough to—"

Bryony laid a hand on Maria's shoulder and closed her eyes, opening them again with a look like Job's when another trial showed up. "How can you be so fearless when it comes to treating your patients, but frozen in your own life?"

"Thanks for the diagnosis. Now tell me why you've come."

"Like I said, to help you. Mom and I talked. You need help. People always want a clown, and I know how to position myself at this time of year. Kelly the Klown takes a bit of the tension and the anticipation off Santa. I'm a regular pressure valve."

Maria laughed. "Two grand statements in the space of a moment."

"It's the entertainer in me." Bryony went to

the laptop she'd set up on the table. "I've made a list of the day cares and private schools in town. They always let me put up flyers. Sometimes I get a job just by talking to the owners and the teachers."

"You probably shouldn't mention my name. Especially at the day care. Jake's daughter works at one and I don't want her to know he was here last night."

"Are you kidding?" While she talked, she whirled around the kitchen, dishing up casserole and biscuits. "I'll be sure not to mention Jake, but I'm going to rehabilitate you. Kelly wouldn't love a bad-girl sister."

Maria stared at the plate Bryony plunked in front of her. "I love you."

"Of course you do."

"I want you to stay, and it's not just because you can cook." She continued around a bite of biscuit. "You're always on my side."

"Isn't this Jake on your side? If not—"

"But don't you have friends who'll expect you for Christmas?" Maria cut her sister off. She'd already covered the "if" in her head. Over and over.

Bryony donned the patient look of Job again. "I know it's not our way, but maybe you could consider me and the rent I'm going to pay you as a character-building exercise. You shrinks should embrace those. I'm one more life-changing event for you this Christmas."

"Thank you. I'm only beginning to realize I need to change my life."

AT THE LUNCH BREAK, Jake ran his aunt's medication over to her and then did a slow roll past Maria's house. He hadn't shared his concern over last night's bang on the door, but he wanted to make sure Maria and her sister were safe.

After court, the last call he made that day was to Tom Drake. The sheriff picked up his own phone. "Don't tell me you've found something we missed in Griff's files," he said.

"No." Maria would laugh at him for believing he could have worked such a miracle. "I have a favor to ask."

"Another one? At least you're asking, rather than ripping a new—"

"Tom, I'm serious."

"What do you need, Jake?"

"I want to talk to Griff's aunt and uncle."

"Not a chance. That kid had a trial."

"I didn't question him."

"If Daley let the people down, that's the breaks of the system. I don't even have legal grounds to bring Butler in."

"Yeah." Jake tapped the top of his desk, his neat blotter, fancy pens and lack of clutter suddenly giving him a view of himself through Leila's eyes. Maybe through Maria's. For longer than he could remember, structure had mattered more to him than the messes that people made.

Not anymore.

"How about a patrol, Tom?"

"On Griff and his family? Are you kidding? We don't have enough budget problems without being sued for harassment?"

"Someone either beat on Maria Keaton's door or threw something at it last—" No need to expose her to chitchat over the police scanner. "Yesterday. I couldn't find anything out there, but the sound was threatening, and I'm concerned for her."

"Why'd she call you, Jake? Her phone doesn't dial nine-one-one?"

"Why are you arguing with every suggestion I make? Just schedule the drive-by. Make sure the kid stays on his own property. Or off hers."

"Why not patrol her house?"

"Because even though half the town suspects her, I think Griff's the only one crazy enough to hurt her, Sheriff. I'd rather know where he is than have him surprise her. Wouldn't we afford anyone in Honesty this small amount of protection?"

"Jake, I'm telling you this as a friend. You need to get yourself under control. I'm starting to think this Keaton woman's as bad as Buck Collier said."

"I'd better be the only person you say that to, Tom."

"Yes, sir."

From the courthouse, Jake went to his own home and packed a small bag. Just for tonight, he told himself. He'd gone out of his way to help both defendants and victims who'd appeared before him in court. He'd arranged drug rehab or bought groceries. He'd pressured landlords who didn't believe in roof repair and he'd sent child protection officers to homes they'd previously ignored.

This was no different. If no one came pounding on Maria's door tonight, he'd go home, and that would be that.

According to Jake's aunt Helen, Maria usually left early in the morning and made a full-time job of looking for work. She answered when he rang her bell and stared at the bag in his right hand.

"I'm not assuming," he said, as her expression was no mystery. "I'll sleep on the couch."

She obviously believed that as much as he did. She looked at him as though she also feared he was out of control.

"What about Leila?" Maria folded her arms across her chest. "What if someone notices you coming out of my house tomorrow morning? How will you explain?"

A movement over Maria's shoulder caught his eye, and then a clown took shape in the semidark hall. He laughed at Bryony's banana-yellow hair and jumper and her regulation white face. Her large, painted mouth, a serious and somehow malevolent line, made him understand close up why Leila had screamed her way through countless birthday parties.

"What?" Maria looked, and then gasped, backing into him. "Bryony, how many times have I begged you not to do that?"

"So I need a real smile?"

"Unless you want to create future therapy opportunities for me," Maria said.

"It could be good for business," Jake said, his hand heavy and warm on her shoulder.

"Kelly the Klown has always been the stuff of my nightmares." Maria pushed the front door shut. "But Bryony's also a marketing genius. She picked up a couple of parties today."

"Your daughter helped me get one gig," Bryony said.

"My daughter? Leila? She share's Dr. Keaton's feelings about clowns."

"But her day care hired Bryony for day after tomorrow," Maria said. "A party to help kick off the holiday season."

Swirling in a whisper of clown costume, Bryony flounced back down the hall. "I guess I'll try on the happy face, but I prefer this one."

"Bryony scares the crap out of me every time she puts on Kelly the Klown." Maria took his bag and set it beside the couch. "It must be the makeup."

"From all that talk in court, I thought nothing scared you." This new information fascinated him. He'd been afraid for her today when he was pushing Tom around.

Worry shadowed her eyes. "I get scared," she said. "I've made a habit of wearing clothes, and I don't require three squares total, but regular meals are a feature of life."

"It's going to be okay," Jake said, even though he couldn't know that. Even though he felt as guilty as if he had called the board and brought this problem to her door.

Maria smiled into his eyes. She tucked his arm close to her side. He felt like groaning at the thrust of her breasts.

"I missed you, too," she said.

"I can stay?" He was relieved he wouldn't have to be all alpha male with her.

"Bryony thinks I turn my back on people to prove I'm strong."

"Who knew a canary-yellow clown could be a font of wisdom?" He pulled his arm free to hug her as he fumbled for his phone. "I should call Leila."

"Is something up with her?" Maria asked.

"No," he said casually. Whether he yelled Tom down or caused havoc in Maria's life with the certainty he was right, he had insecurities of his own. "Ever since I found out about the cutting, I call her every night, usually right before I leave the office. If she doesn't hear from me, she might wonder. She might think I've regressed, and I'm not ever going to live-and-let-live with Leila again."

"But won't she ask where you are?"

"I didn't plan to tell her, but she'll guess I'm not camping by the lake in November." He shut his phone. "You're right. I should probably talk to her in person, if she'll open the door."

"You're asking for a fight if you confide in Leila."

"If I'm honest with my daughter, the one thing I haven't been all her life? From what she says, another lie will be the end of us."

"Ever since we started—whatever this is— you've been trying to make sure Leila didn't find out. And I thought that was wise. Why the sudden change of heart?"

"Why are you suddenly so worried? Because it might not last?"

Her brittle smile challenged him. He took her shoulders. "I didn't stay with you last night because I was curious," he said, "and it wasn't a one-night thing. I've had that, and I don't need more. I need you. If it ends, that's one thing, but no matter what happens with your job, and this Griff situation, I'm going to want to be with you."

"Do you know how Leila feels about the divorce?"

"You don't have to hint that she feels betrayed. I got that from her, but I'm not going back to Kate, and I don't want Leila to find out I'm with you from someone else. I should have told her today, in case someone did see me leave this morning."

Maria locked her fingers together. "It's a mistake."

"Telling Leila doesn't lock you into a relationship you don't want, Maria."

"I want you," she said, her savage tone startling him—distracting him.

He quirked a finger under her chin and kissed her, lingering over her soft lips, glad for the strength in her hand as she cradled his nape. He lifted his head with reluctance. Touching her at all was torture when he had to leave.

"I'm not taking an ad out in your newspaper," he said, smiling against her lips. "I'm telling my daughter I'm interested in a woman before she hears gossip."

"The wrong woman. I'm supposed to be her doctor."

"You know that's over," he said. "It's too late for us to stop. Whatever is between us is going to happen." He glanced down the hall. Somewhere farther inside the house, Bryony was making noise—cooking, doing dishes, maybe boiling up something to use as part of her clown getup. "I'll only be gone a few minutes, and then we can discuss this in more privacy if you want."

"I'm not trying to create drama, and I don't want to hurt Leila, but I think you're going too far."

"You're concerned for her." He shook his head. "And maybe you're feeling a bit tender." He cleared his throat, which suddenly felt tight. "But I'm Leila's father. I'm trying to do the right thing for her, too."

Maria gnawed at her cheek. "Maybe you're right. I wish I could speak to her."

At that, he hugged her and left. There wasn't much he could say about Maria's suspension.

He drove to Leila's town house. Her lights were on, but she didn't answer her doorbell.

Women.

He dialed Leila's number. She didn't answer her phone, either. The call rolled over to voice mail.

"Leila, it's Dad. I just wanted to let you know I won't be at home." He swallowed, his mouth dry. "We should talk about it. Call me when you can. I love you."

He hung up but waited in his car, hoping his daughter would pick up his message and come to the door.

She didn't. She might be even more temperamental and stubborn than the other woman on his mind. She might have more reason.

After about ten minutes, he drove back to Maria's. She also seemed uncertain whether to answer her door, but at last it swung back, revealing her in pajama bottoms and a tank. Need for her roared to life. All it took was a glimpse of striped cotton slung low on her narrow hips, and her full, pointed breasts stretching the tee.

"Did she speak to you?" Maria asked.

For a second, he actually had to wonder who she meant. "No," he said, sounding hoarse even to himself. "She didn't answer the door or the phone."

"I'm sorry." Maria had lit a fire in the large stone fireplace, and she led him to the sofa. As they sat, she leaned into him and he pulled her across his chest. "Really, I'm sorry, even though I made a fuss."

"I agree with everything you said, and I don't want you to feel tied to me." More than part of him wondered if that was the biggest lie he'd ever told. She raised anxious eyes. "I want you to feel safe," he said. "With me. Not rushed."

"Did you tell Leila she could find you here?"

He shook his head.

"Why not?"

"I didn't want to leave that information in a phone message." He kissed her temple, breathing in her scent.

"I know." She lifted her head. "That makes sense. But are you sure that's the only reason?"

"What do you mean?"

"Are you worried about how she'll take the news of us seeing each other?"

"A little," he said. "But I believe in my daughter. And you can believe in me."

"Trust isn't my strongest trait right now."

"Time will show you I'm safe to trust," he said, trying not to be frustrated. He cupped her breast, and his arousal could have left her in no doubt about his feelings tonight. "I want to be with you." Beneath his thumb, her nipple puckered, and her breathing grew ragged.

She met his gaze with the hunger he wanted to slake. "I'm sorry I'm acting like this. It's not me."

"Maybe you're afraid." He was. He'd never cared like this. He'd never acted out of character for any woman before, and yet here he was, filled with doubts and bullying Tom Drake, who'd never been anything but a friend.

"Maybe you're right." Passion curved her mouth as she opened her arms to him. "I'm afraid because I care about you, and we're moving too fast in a situation that isn't normal."

Behind her, Bryony pranced into the hall, bedecked in a new purple costume with a massive frilly collar. He let Maria go, and she backed away immediately, but Bryony darted back into her room, with a laughing "Sorry."

"Oh my God," Maria said. "You can't imagine how bad this is."

"I don't care," he said. "Bryony, at least, won't be traumatized. Come to bed."

As they reached Maria's bedroom, he was already tugging her tank top over her head. She shut her door and then reached for his belt buckle. He sucked in his stomach.

"This feels so good, it has to be wrong," she said, pressing her breasts to his chest.

"You're out of your mind." He caught the nape of her neck and kissed her with the hunger that had grown out of twelve or so hours of not holding her.

She undid his zipper. Her hands, sliding inside his waistband, were cool and strong and drove him insane.

"I thought women liked foreplay," he said.

"I'm sure we'll need it someday. Right now, I just need you."

THE NEXT MORNING, Maria awoke in the early dark, doubts coming back in full force.

With bare-naked need, she smoothed Jake's dark curls over his forehead. His eyes flickered. He caught her hand and kissed her palm, his mouth opening just enough to destroy her will to leave.

"I don't like being late," she said. "Especially not two days in a row."

"For the paper route?" He laughed, stretching his long, gorgeous body. "I'll wait here." He folded her fingers and kissed her knuckles. "Wake me when you get back."

"All speed records for paper folding will fall today."

She went to her appointed corner, trying not to analyze where she might be headed with a business-first, justice-oriented, no-feelings-allowed guy. Well, she conceded, that last part was untrue. He obviously had feelings.

She didn't notice the newspaper photo at first. She was inserting flyers for roasting hens and "green" cleaners when she recognized Jake wearing only his pants. She dropped the flyers and moved under the streetlight, staring at the back of the *Sentinel*'s first section in horror.

Honesty's only paper had a tiny gossip page. Most folks liked to cover the good stuff face-to-face, over a back fence or a coffeehouse counter. But Honesty was also a microcosm of the bigger world, and the small section usually covered fundraisers or who was sexing it up with whom—relayed in subtle hints.

Jake hadn't received the benefit of even a bludgeoning hint.

Someone had been outside Maria's house when Bryony had arrived. Someone who'd taken a picture of exactly the moment that had stopped Bryony in her tracks.

The photo had caught Maria standing just in front of Jake, not quite covering up the fact that he was nearly naked in her open doorway.

She felt sick, but the *Sentinel* editor must have felt the people of Honesty needed to know how a steadfast judge spent his time with a recently disgraced psychologist who'd clearly made the most of her visit to his courtroom.

CHAPTER FOURTEEN

TEARS OF SHAME scalded Maria's eyes as she scanned the brief article on her part in getting Griff acquitted. Not even Beth Nikolas would be able to respect her now. Without exactly saying it, the article managed to imply exactly what she'd feared, that she'd lost her job for good and was making do with Jake.

He'd be lucky to salvage his own career now.

She swore and folded the papers even faster. Delivering them was like stabbing Jake in the heart over and over again. She was grateful for the cover of a dark morning as she made her way back home.

She scooped her paper out of the holly bush beside her front porch and carried it inside. Still in her coat and gloves, she opened her bedroom door.

Jake came out of the bathroom in another towel, his face swathed in shaving cream. "You did break records."

"I have to show you something. You need to go to Leila before she sees it."

"What?"

She held out the paper. While he read the article, she got another towel and handed it to him when he came after her into the bathroom.

"Are you all right?" he asked.

"What about you? You'll be lucky if the town doesn't find a rail built for two. I know I inserted flyers for tar and feathers this morning."

"That's real funny." Jake avoided her glance as he wiped shaving cream off his face. "Will you come with me to talk to Leila?"

Maria stared at him in the mirror, but he wouldn't meet her gaze. Showing uncharacteristic vulnerability, he seemed fascinated by the foam that had dripped to the edge of the sink. He looked up so suddenly, his dark expression startled Maria.

"I'm not asking you because I'm afraid to talk to Leila," he said. "But I am afraid for her. You'll be able to tell if she—"

"You didn't ask me along last night."

"Because I wanted to be the one to tell her and you're not supposed to see her. I wasn't being outed by the local newspaper."

"I—" If she went, it could mean the end of her license. She tried to look into Jake's eyes.

"I know I can never treat Leila again, but the Psychology Review Board doesn't. I'm afraid if I go with you now, I'll never be able to treat anyone else again, either."

"You're saying no?"

"No." It wasn't in her, but to give up everything she'd worked for… "I could offer you the names of the same therapists I recommended to her."

"The ones she refuses to see?"

Silence filled her bathroom and the lengthening space between them. She watched as he reached for his pants. She cared about Leila, and that photo was going to be a blow. The younger woman had never even been able to admit aloud that she wished her parents would find a way back to each other. Seeing her father in such a compromising position with Maria would hurt her.

"Okay," she said. "As soon as you dress." She moved to the bathroom door and clung to the jamb for dear life. "You look as if you're sorry, as if we made a mistake."

"I'm sorry for you." He turned away as he dropped the towel and began to dress. In the past two days, they'd shared their bodies the way they'd shared her quilt and late-night snacks from the fridge and one pillow in the middle of her bed. But it seemed that was all over now.

The fruit of the tree of knowledge had dropped on their heads. "And Leila," Jake said. "This is going to hurt both of you."

"And you. Being with me puts your career in jeopardy."

"You're sorry?" he asked.

"I am now." She turned away, but let him catch her arm.

"What are you thinking, Maria?"

"Same as you. Keeping our distance would have been the safer, wiser move." She laughed, seeing nothing funny in their so-called relationship. "You don't respect us in the morning."

"Respect? What are you talking about?" But he turned away to button his shirt, too.

Neither could face the other.

"It's okay." It wasn't. It was anything but. Yet, she couldn't bring herself to ask outright for reassurance about the respect and intimacy that had linked them the past two nights. Had she imagined the connection that had made her sleep happily in his arms?

Happiness and safety—two things she'd never depended on anyone else to give her.

"I'm sorry someone took that picture," he said. "And I'd like to ask the editor why he thought it was newsworthy. I'm not sorry about—" She tried to back into her bedroom, but he caught her arms. "I'm not sorry about being with you. How do I convince you?"

"Get your shoes," she said, her voice a rasp. "We should take the paper along, and we have to hurry. Leila's working the early morning hours at the day care this term, and she opens up. We need to catch her at home."

Jake touched her face, his fingers gentle. His eyes were kind but hollow. "Why do you assume we're over?"

"That's a problem I have, left over from a long time ago. I tend to believe people I care for are going to flee."

Jake leaned down. His lips against her temple were warm. The scent of shaving cream and clean male made her want to lean against him, but a last stubborn vestige of caution stopped her.

The kiss was apparently supposed to ease her confusion, despite the silence between them. After a few seconds, she wrapped her arms around him and hugged tight before pulling abruptly away. It was as close as she would ever come to asking him to care for her.

"Let's drive," Jake said, buttoning his shirt. "I'd hate to see her pass us as we're walking to her place."

Fine. Less time to think or talk. All good. For both of them.

Awkwardness spiked the silence while they drove to Leila's town house. As they climbed the icy steps to the small porch, Maria's heart banged in her chest like a ball bearing in a pinball machine. Before they could ring the bell, Leila snatched the door open, as if she'd been watching for them.

To Maria's surprise, Jake twined his fingers with hers. She shivered and saw Leila stare at their hands. Maria couldn't stop herself from pulling away.

"Don't you think it's a little late to hide what you've been doing with my father, Doctor?" Her sarcasm was a bitter cloud.

"Let me explain," Jake said.

Leila raked them each with an icicle glance and then reached behind her. She turned back with a coat and her purse. "How many times have I prayed you'd say that to me, Dad? You keep making decisions that turn my life upside down, and I still don't know why you threw my mother out."

"This has nothing to do with your mother, and that photo doesn't tell you everything."

Maria opened her mouth, but Jake took her hand again, a clear warning in his too-firm grip. She stared at him. What next?

Leila burned Maria with a glance. "Back

then, I wanted to know what was going on in our own house. At least you don't have to explain what's been happening with my psychologist." She grabbed the paper from his free hand and banged her purse against the photo. "Everything's there for the whole town to see. In black-and-white pixels."

"I want to explain," Jake said. "Everything."

"I said you don't have to. Who were you sleeping with when you got tired of Mom?"

"Leila, you know me," Jake said, his voice harsh with pain and truth. "I wouldn't do that."

"I don't know you or Mom. I don't know what happened to us, and Maria, I don't get how you can jump into bed with my father. Are you trying to bribe him into talking to that board?"

Maria sucked in a shocked breath. Jake stepped forward.

"No," he said. "Stay mad at me, Leila. I deserve it, but Maria wouldn't use me."

"What can I believe except what they say in there?" She slapped at the paper in her father's hand. "I don't know why you came over here anyway, and I'm busy."

"Call your boss. We have to talk this out," Jake said.

"I don't want to see either of you. Ever." Maria had been afraid Leila might try to hide her feelings, but they spilled into the cold air. Leila pushed between them onto the sidewalk, but Jake went after her.

He skidded around Leila on the ice, managing to stop in front of her. "I don't blame you for feeling betrayed, but I tried to call you last night."

"I won't start cutting myself again over your affair with my therapist," Leila said, and Maria found her heartfelt disgust almost a relief. "Get out of my way, Dad."

"I will." He didn't. "I love you, Leila. I stayed with your mother when our marriage was long since over because I love you. I will never stop loving you, no matter how many mistakes I make. If you have to hate me, that's your choice, but it won't stop me loving you."

"And that's supposed to make me—what?"

He finally took a step back, his intensity softening into confusion. "Remember that I love you," he said. "One day, when you need to count on me."

"Right. I don't see that day coming." She continued down the sidewalk to her car. She opened the door and started to get in, but straightened. "Dr. Keaton?"

"Yes?" Maria said, bracing herself.

"You're fired."

MARIA WAS SHOVELING her walk two days later when two wolfhounds dragged their silver-haired owner down the frozen sidewalk. Helen Sloane, Jake's aunt, being walked by her dogs.

Maria bit her lip. It wasn't safe, but if she were seventysomething, she'd resent a younger woman suggesting she couldn't handle her own pups.

Maria had minded her own business instead of offering Helen Sloane help for months. Now that she'd put the finger of guilt on Jake's bare chest in the morning newspaper, it was a bad time to change her approach.

But the ice and the dogs were a lethal combination. And it wasn't just because her feelings for Jake made her feel connected to his family, too.

"Excuse me, Mrs. Sloane," she said.

"Whoa," the lady called to her charges. "Madden, Montana, slow it down before you break my hip."

Since she'd mentioned it first... "Can I help?" Maria asked. "I'd be happy to walk your dogs for you."

"I beg your pardon," Mrs. Sloane said as her dogs sniffed anxiously at Maria's ankles. "I'm perfectly capable of caring for my animals."

"Of course, but the weather's cold." Maria danced out of the reach of one long snout, only to find herself close up with the other. "I've just given up my gym membership, and I could use the exercise."

"I couldn't pay you much," Helen said, while she looked as if she were calculating in her head.

"Pay me? I'm offering a favor," Maria said. One of the dogs gave a high-pitched yelp that probably shattered several windows. "Don't worry about money."

"Oh, no." Helen Sloane yanked the leashes out of Maria's reach. "I love my babies, but I know they're wild boys. I can't let you walk them if you won't let me pay you."

"We're neighbors."

"Let's be businesslike. I have a need, and I know myself. If I let you walk Montana and Madden once, I won't be able to resist using you again."

"I'd be glad to do it until the weather improves."

"Businesslike obviously won't work, so I'll try bluntness." Helen waggled the leashes, offering the temptation of employment, however ungainful. "My nephew tells me you're looking all over town for work."

"Jake asked you to help me?"

"Don't be upset with him. We got frank with each other after I told him off for letting some sniper with a camera get a shot of him apparently exiting your bedroom."

"Oh, God."

"Pray for your sins later. Let's talk terms."

Maria considered getting sick on the woman's sturdy boots instead.

"Come on, girl. You're no wilting lily."

"Oh, yeah." She might be. "What kind of pay are we talking?" Maria patted one aristocratic, canine head. "Is this Madden?" The yelper.

"And the other one's Montana. I name my dogs after the figures in the glory years of football."

Maria had no idea whom she meant, but she smiled as if she understood. "They're beautiful. You take good care of them."

"It's a constant effort. I even have to wipe them down after walks because they loll about and get themselves filthy. Maybe I could engage you to bathe them, as well?"

"Sure. I might as well rob you blind all at once. You already know my name is Maria?"

"You're my own Christmas elf." The woman stuck out her hand. "Helen Sloane."

"Do you prefer Mrs. Sloane?"

"Helen." They shook. "I'm thinking forty dollars a week," she said. "Three walks per day, a bath each week, and emergency baths if they manage to escape you and paddle in a puddle."

"I'm thinking forty dollars is way too much." To her shame, she found herself wishing she could add forty dollars a week to the meager lines in her household budget. "How about twenty?"

"I like thirty."

"Twenty-five?"

"Thirty, or I'll know you're just showing an old woman pity."

Maria hesitated. She'd prefer not to mug a woman who had both a need for digitalis and a fixed income. As if to help her decide, Madden and Montana yanked at their leashes and bolted.

Maria ran after them and their mistress, a little concerned the "babies" might have jolted Helen's shoulders out of their sockets.

"Deal," Maria said, swooping around Helen to take the dogs in hand. If they didn't cost her thirty dollars' worth of effort, she'd give the extra to Jake and force him to take it back to his aunt. "I'll start right now."

"Excellent." Helen handed over the leashes with alacrity. "I'll walk with you today, and you can tell me about Griff Butler."

"I'd rather not."

"I'm a fixture in this community. I can help you."

"I don't need help."

"Don't kid yourself. You and Jake would both be hot topics around the water coolers if anyone still had them. No, Griff is the subject we need to discuss. You certainly didn't seduce that young man?"

"Hell, no." Maria looked down. "Sorry. I mean no, I didn't."

"Your first answer works for me. It's just the way I would respond. How did this happen?"

Helen seemed to assume she had the right to know about Maria's personal life. "I don't mean to offend you, but we hardly know each other, and I don't need thirty dollars enough to talk about Griff Butler."

"Nonsense. We've been nodding to each other on the sidewalk for over a year. You need a friend."

"A paying one?" Maria asked.

"I know you haven't seen my nephew in two days, because he told me he doesn't want to expose you to more ridicule." Helen touched Maria's hand. "Perhaps you miss him?"

"I don't want to," she said, her heartfelt admission husky with emotion.

"Jake also says you're reluctant to talk about the things that matter to you. You have that in common with him. He's staying away to give you time and respectability, but he believes you'll think he's avoiding you to regain his dignity."

"He doesn't sound reluctant about talking." Unlike Jake, she didn't plan to confide her deepest, darkest secrets to his candid aunt. "My sister is staying with me right now, so I can tell her everything I don't want to say to you."

When Helen laughed, the dogs began snapping at each other. Maria used their leashes to steer them apart, and they quickly fell into companionable step again.

"I've annoyed you, but let me tell you what Jake's feeling."

"Did he hire you to act as his matchmaker?"

Helen turned, her face alight as if they'd shared a moment of pure understanding. "That was my idea, but he asked me to stay out of the personal matters between you. Still, he doesn't always know best, so I'll tell you what I think he would say if he could. That he hasn't stayed away because he doesn't want to see you. That the only thing he wants more is not to hurt you."

Maria watched her own feet scuff down the sidewalk.

"You know I'm safe to talk to because my nephew has shared his heartfelt secrets with me." Helen smoothed the scarf at her throat. "Well, in all honesty, he didn't say those things out loud, but I know what he's feeling. That boy has been like a son to me."

Boy? Maria kept walking.

"Maybe I should guess at your feelings for him, as well?"

Oh. No. "Why do you want to know about Griff?"

Madden intervened again, veering toward a holly bush strewn with lights that barely sparkled during the day.

"Someone's going to have an impressive power bill." Dragging at Madden's leash, Maria hoped to distract Helen. The dog got back into step with Montana.

Helen would not be deterred. "Let's talk straight. I don't know what you did with that boy Griff, but I love my nephew, and I think he's getting involved with you."

Staying at her side, Maria crunched through a few steps of frozen snow in silence. She cared for Jake, more than she was willing to say. More than she was willing to discuss with his aunt, for sure.

"I won't do anything to hurt Jake." She looked into the other woman's clear gray eyes. "And I know I've hurt Leila by letting myself get—" She couldn't come up with words to describe what was going on between her and Jake. She'd never felt so attached so quickly. She'd never been so physically involved, but she hadn't totally lost her mind. She'd made love with him despite her commitment to Leila, and that was out of character. "I should have put her first."

"I went straight to her when Jake told me how fed up she is with the pair of you. While I wish you'd both realized she had prior claims on both of you, I think you did her a favor. She might finally be angry enough to get better."

"You knew she was ill?"

"Not the extent of it, but she was obviously troubled after her parents' divorce. Kate was too self-absorbed to notice, and I think Jake was too frightened to stop being blind."

Maria didn't want to know anything else about Jake's failed marriage with the infamous Kate, but she was anxious enough about Leila to trust Helen's judgment. "You're sure she's not putting on a front for you?"

"I'm checking in with her often." Helen reached for a length of Montana's leash when he went for a blow-up Santa. "I know you don't know me, but you need me, too, Maria. What you should have done from the start was approach some member of the community to act on your behalf."

"A PR move?" Maria asked, smiling despite her confusion at Helen's whirlwind recitation of solutions to all her problems.

"I don't think it's too late for me to do you some good. Tell me about Griff." Helen put up one hand in her creamy, knit glove. "Jake tells me you'd rather eat dirt than accept help. It's time to get out your fork and spoon."

Somehow Helen the Maelstrom worked up enough patience to wait while Maria found the courage to speak, but Maria had underestimated the relief she'd find in pouring out the whole story.

Helen didn't judge. She walked along, making appropriate shocked noises when the time was right. "You cannot blame yourself for what's happened with this boy, or even for the—hopefully—temporary loss of your clients. What would you do differently if you could go back and do it again?"

"That is a damn good question, Helen." She stopped. "Oh, sorry for the language."

Helen gave an eye roll that would have done a teenager proud. "Please, young lady. As if I never heard that word before. I say it every time I try to find my glasses in the morning. Go on with your thought."

"I had no choice with Griff. I hope all my clients are seeing other therapists and moving ahead, but I wouldn't have let him get away with murder just to be available for the others."

"At last you let your halo slip long enough to be annoyed with that kid."

"I've got no halo," she said indignantly. Helen merely laughed, and Maria found herself laughing, too. The sound ricocheted between the snowy houses.

"So your only option now is to move forward, as well."

"I'm trying, but I'm running out of money, and I miss my work. I have no idea how long the board's going to take with their investigation."

"I'm suggesting you stop hiding out with paper routes. Take dog walking or any other job until the community is willing to forgive."

Maria knew good advice when she heard it, though its rightness made it no easier to follow. "I've just embarked on my dog-walking career. And even though almost no one in this town will hire me, I'll find other things. I have to."

"Try not to worry," Helen said. "Isn't that what you'd suggest to anyone who came to you for help with similar issues? You're looking for work. You've done all you could to help that boy. Time is the only certainty you can count on to help you."

"I don't know, Helen. You're a bit of a Christmas present."

A WEEK AFTER he'd last seen Maria, Jake came up with a plan. Helen refused to share the gist of her conversations with the woman who occupied most of his thoughts and all his sleepless nights.

The most she'd let slip was Maria's preoccupation with foreclosure and financial ruin.

He wasn't allowed to interfere with the board's investigation, but he made up his mind to find more work for Maria.

Without telling Helen what was on his mind, he shoveled her walk, and then he took care of three of her closest friends' snow, as well. After he finished each job, he knocked on the owner's door.

Janet Loomis and Delilah Cantrell showed amazing restraint in not interrogating him about his recent newspaper fame. They even agreed to let Aunt Helen persuade Maria to take over the snow-shoveling job. Strong-arming them into letting him pay Maria through them was tougher, but he could hardly let them foot the bill for his own bright ideas.

Sam Burke, on Helen's other side, proved testy when Jake suggested Maria could shovel his walk, too. "Isn't that the girl who blamed the Butler boy for killing his parents?"

"She's the woman who was treating him for his problems when he confessed to her," Jake said.

"I've known the Butlers forever. They don't have that kind of blood."

"That's not the way it works, Sam."

"Yeah, well, I'm not sure I can betray the

family." He looked Jake up and down. "No matter what you're getting out of the deal."

Jake considered shoving his aunt's senior citizen friend headfirst into a snowbank. Hardly the right thing to do.

"Sam, you won't betray anyone if you let me pay Maria for shoveling your walk. For all we know, it may not snow again, and the question won't come up."

"That's true," said Sam Burke, still good-old-boyish enough to fall in with another of Honesty's oldest families. "I reckon you have a soft spot for that girl?"

"Woman," Jake said. "Doctor. I mean, Sam, it's none of your business."

"Son, you've made it everyone's business."

"Which is why I'm trying to make amends. Do you know anyone else who needs some odd jobs done around the house?"

"I saw Pete Donelly out chipping at his birdbath the other day. You know, he's in that house catty-corner behind mine."

"I know Pete." And he just had time to stop by before he went to Leila's town house and begged her again to talk to him.

Maybe the Fates would be kind. After all, he was trying everything to make reparation for his sins.

WITH NO WARNING AT ALL, Maria found people calling her to do their chores. They must have seen her walking Helen's dogs. And she was able to do all the jobs—filling bird feeders and cleaning a birdbath, rebuilding a doghouse, even painting a mailbox, out in the open like any other citizen of Honesty. She never met one accusing eye.

Unlike Jake, whose every case seemed to be under review in the paper and on each unguarded tongue.

Maria heard about this case being rethought or that charge being re-argued while she was working. She'd been in the feed store, picking up birdseed when she'd overheard the two men in front of her at the checkout discussing a burglary case.

"I heard there were questions about the evidence. Maybe he sided with one of the defendants in that case, too."

"She wasn't a defendant. She just should have been."

"I'd put myself through law school if I thought someone would present their case to me the way she's doing with him."

As the men had shared horselike snickers, she'd eased her bags back onto the shelf and left to buy her birdseed at the discount store on the edge of town.

Every day, she tried a little harder to let the future take care of itself. Her job prospects sucked, but present conditions, if she didn't count an uncomfortable, ungovernable, constant ache for Jake, were looking up.

Helen knew everyone in town, and she'd apparently hit them all up for their small jobs. None of it would pay the cable bill, so Maria had turned off the cable, despite Bryony's certainty that her creativity would dry right up if she couldn't watch reality programs on MTV, fix-it-yourself shows on several home-oriented channels and cooking on nearly all the others.

Working should have kept Maria's mind occupied, but Jake inveigled his way into every other thought. Jake, worrying about Leila, who wouldn't speak to either of them. Jake, promising never to cause her pain, and yet never showing up again—though Helen had pointed out a sudden prevalence of police patrols on their street.

After a typical day of delivering papers, shoveling walks, walking dogs and facing down any angry citizen who frowned at her, Maria went home and showered off the grime.

The phone rang as she was drying her hair.

She checked the caller ID, shamelessly hoping to see Jake's name, but it was A. Hammond.

Maria barely got out a hello before a woman began to spew.

"Thanks to that picture and the foul way you live your life, I've just made sure you'll never hurt another child. Or an adult, for that matter. The only license you'll get is one you print yourself. And I wouldn't put that past you."

Her hysterical voice sent a shiver down Maria's spine. "Who is this?"

"Angela Hammond. And another thing, I want you to keep that judge away from my house and my family. If he comes near us again, I'll have him picked up by his friend the sheriff."

The judge? Jake. "Angela Hammond? Griff's aunt?" The pieces began to mesh, though she couldn't believe Jake would take matters into his own hands after she'd begged him not to. "I don't understand what you're saying." Worse than that, she didn't want to believe Jake still didn't know when to stay out of a situation he couldn't fix.

"Don't try to play me. I made an appointment with that review board the day Buck Collier told me he'd reported you. Then your photo with the damn judge on Griff's case landed on my doorstep. I'll see you in hell or in jail before you ever treat another person in Honesty. I told those other doctors everything they needed to know about you and your lover boy."

A knot of anger toward Buck and Angela and every other narrow-minded soul in this town made speech difficult. "You talked to the board." Surely they'd recognize her poison for what it was.

"I told them everything."

"Everything Griff told you."

"Exactly. I gave them the truth, and about damn time someone did." Mrs. Hammond finished the conversation by calling her several names that Maria prayed she'd used with the investigators so they'd realize the woman was grinding an ax as sharp as her temper.

While Maria was gathering a breath to ask when Jake had visited their home, the other woman slammed down the phone. The metallic thud echoed in Maria's ear. She hung up and dropped into an armchair.

Jake hadn't helped with his good-intentional meddling. But the board couldn't take the word of a woman so obviously biased. Surely she'd be offered the chance to defend herself.

No wonder Jake had avoided her. He'd done exactly what she'd asked him not to, and he'd pushed her several steps closer to ruin.

Maria stood and yanked the living room

curtains shut. Jake couldn't help himself. If his perception of the right thing required tearing down the world, he pitched in with both hands, and to hell with the fallout.

She slumped onto the love seat's ottoman, her head in her hands. Forcing herself to breathe slowly, all she could see was Jake at his most remote, bent on doing what he deemed best, no matter what she asked of him.

She picked up the phone again, uncertain whether she wanted him to offer an acceptable excuse, or warn him that Griff's aunt would probably find someone willing to censure him, as well.

Maria set down the phone. This conversation would be better held in person. She hurried to her room and changed, before grabbing her keys and running for the car. She'd never been inside Jake's beautiful brick house on the hill above Honesty. She rang the bell, her heart thumping.

He answered, his face darkening in a way she already recognized. "God, I'm glad to see you."

"You won't be." Landscaping shielded them from the quiet street at the end of his curved driveway. "May I come in?"

He scooped her inside with one arm, all but lifting her off her feet. His mouth brushed hers, and she lifted her arms before she remembered the reason she'd come. "Angela Hammond called me."

He caught her hand as she tried to twist away from him. "I thought she might," he said. "I should have called you first."

"You must have been busy."

"Why are you angry, Maria?"

He shut the door. It echoed in his long, arched hallway. Cold from his marble floor all but crept through the soles of her boots. Unless it was the cold drifting down from her heart. Jake's bewilderment was in character, but ridiculous. He actually thought they could pick up where they'd left off, even though he'd been avoiding her since the newspaper debacle.

"How could you talk to Griff's family?"

"I've read his police file, and the school counselor got in touch after she saw that newspaper article. She thought you and I might be on the same side, so she told me I should talk to the principal. Griff has bullied some younger children, vandalized a couple of classrooms. He stole computer equipment he didn't even need. His parents and his aunt found excuses for him. For your sake, as well as his, someone had to talk to his aunt about his propensity for violence."

"You were the wrong choice," Maria said. "And I begged you not to."

"Come into the study. Sit down and I'll bring you something to drink. We'll talk."

"No." She put a round marble-topped table between them, ignoring all the doors set into the paneled walls. "When we get too cozy—" could anyone get cosy in this stuffy house? "—I start trusting and stop thinking. I'm beginning to wonder if you're always planning your own strategy, even as you tell me what I want to hear."

"I never lied to you."

"But you didn't tell me everything you've done to 'help' me."

"I didn't speak to Angela Hammond to stir her up against you. The kid needs help, and he's not going back to trial, no matter what."

"You can't stop yourself. Griff may have learned he can get away with murder. I've learned a healthy respect for considering consequences before I put my neck on the line. You continue to believe that you know how to shape the world, and that everyone will realize you were right in the end, and that Leila will forgive you. Griff's aunt and uncle will be glad you either get them killed or get their nephew spotlighted by everyone in authority in his life. And I don't know how you think I'm going to feel about you, or if you even care, but you can't keep managing us all as if you're playing a game and we're your soldiers."

"I don't." His voice was pure Jake, passionate and proud, dismissive of her accusation. He leaned on the other side of the table, his knuckles white, his face drawn. "I wanted to help you. I wanted to protect you. But in the end, that kid and his family needed to understand their own situation."

Maria, rubbed her fist across her forehead. "I'm amazed you can't see that this is the same old, same old."

"I'm not blind."

His pain reached out to her, but she put up her hands to fend him off. "You're driving us both into a situation we can't recover from. Leila's going to be the daughter of a disgraced judge. Think of her if you can't stop saving the world long enough to save yourself."

"How could I avoid doing my duty? Why didn't you just testify to Griff's confession? You jeopardized yourself trying to show the jury that he needed help. Surely you can understand why I had to take the school's information to his aunt and uncle. Wasn't I doing exactly what you did?"

"I learned my lesson the hard way, Jake." She

moved away from the table. "Surely you can see I'm talking about us as much as about Griff. I asked you not to involve yourself in this."

"And I didn't intend to turn Angela Hammond on you, but I had the same choices you did at trial. That family has two small children. If Griff is violent, someone has to help them."

"What happened to your objectivity, Jake?"

"That's what I don't get about this argument. You and Leila keep telling me I have to choose a side. Well, I did, and now I get the feeling you're saying we're over."

"Over?" She stood still. Even when he put his arms around her, she held back. Her heart hurt. "What was there to end? You slept at my house a couple of times. I thought we cared about each other. The paper embarrassed you. You left."

"I stayed away from you because I didn't want to cause any more talk." He held her close enough that she felt his pulse thumping through his shirt. She fought her ridiculous need to forgive and forget. "About you," he said.

"I have to take care of myself now. I have to let the board do their investigation and I need to reopen my practice. I don't need to fight with a man for boundaries that should be second nature to you."

"You sound like a therapist."

"I am one, and the good I can do in my job is as important to me as anything you can do from your seat on the bench."

"So you're dumping me because I tried to help Griff and his family?"

"Stop saying I'm dumping you." She pulled away from him and immediately felt cold without the warmth of his body around her. "You disappeared. You could have called. Instead, you're trying to fix everything behind my back. You want to make the people in this town see that I was right, and that they should accept me again."

"You won't hear me, Maria. I do want you to have everything that matters to you. I'd love to be the one to hand you your life back on a silver platter, but I also had to help that family."

A phone rang somewhere. Jake glanced toward the nearest open door. The phone rang again. He swore softly. "That's not more important than you, but I'm waiting for information on another matter. I have to take it."

"Good luck to you and all your matters." She started for the door. Another matter, indeed.

"Wait," he said, and for once she ducked his reaching hand. "Wait for me. We aren't finished talking." His rich voice rubbed her heart raw with a reminder of the passion she was about to lose.

"Goodbye."

"Not for good, Maria."

The extent of his arrogance startled her. She ran to his front door and managed to drag it open. She was in her car before she looked back, but he hadn't bothered to come after her.

Maria swallowed hot tears as she drove away. She shouldn't have opened that door if she'd wanted him to stop her. She'd never played silly girl games to keep a guy.

She was smarter than this. Leila knew her own father, and Maria had heard all the worst about Jake from Leila. Maria had seen him in action in court and after Griff's verdict. But despite all the evidence, she'd convinced herself she was important enough to Jake to make him stop intervening when intervention was pointless and likely to create more havoc.

She blinked until her view of the road cleared.

It was over. She wouldn't hold Jake again. She wouldn't sleep curled into his body. She wouldn't feel the pressure of his mouth on hers, or give in, joyfully, to the need she could not restrain.

She had to heal, get her own life back on track. Maybe cutting herself off from the man she'd turned to while she'd felt desperate and frightened was a first step. A second step included robbing the teens in this town of all their extra work so she could earn a few extra pennies.

On the bright side, Maria was learning to be grateful for her sister's help. Kelly the Klown had managed to book a party in all the classrooms at Leila's day care center.

Maria often wondered what would have happened if Bryony had introduced herself as Dr. Keaton's sister. Someone would eventually realize that Kelly the Klown was also named Keaton.

At her own front door, Maria hitched the lapels of her coat closed and tried to paint the hurt out of her face. Her sister must have walked in just ahead of her. Still in her silky clown jumper, Bryony carried today's green hair, but she jumped when she saw Maria.

Maria managed a weak laugh. "I scared you for a change?"

"I didn't expect you home already. I'll make dinner tonight."

"Thanks. I'm exhausted. Bird…leavings have twice the strength of industrial-grade glue."

Bryony settled her hair on the newel post. "You're learning to just say okay. I like being the one who helps."

"I'm also starving," Maria said. "Sitting behind a desk isn't manual labor. Lately, I start thinking about what's for dinner as soon as I finish breakfast. Peter gave me a blueberry muffin this afternoon, and I swear my hands shook as I took it."

"You sound chipper."

She must be one of the world's great actresses. "Getting there." She raked her tangled hair over her shoulders. "I am grateful to you, and I'm making friends with the people I work for." She had lots to be grateful for, even if her few days with Jake had been a baffling mistake.

"You weren't friends with that mob before now?"

"I think half of them assumed I was guilty. Helen must be an arm twister worthy of professional wrestling. It's only been a few days, and already that older guy on the other side of her house smiles at me when he opens his door."

"Only you could measure a smile as progress," Bryony said.

"And I could be wrong. They might all be desperate to have their dogs walked and their snow removed. You sound tired."

Bryony reached behind her back for the zipper on her costume. "This was the hardest day yet. One of the kids kind of spooked me."

"Why?"

"He asked me if I was your sister. He said his

mommy told him the clown's sister was a bad lady."

"That's a mood buster. What was his name?"

"These kids don't wear name tags. I'm going to wash off my makeup."

"I'll get changed and make a salad."

She'd just stepped out of the shower when the doorbell rang. Bryony was busy in the kitchen, so Maria quickly threw on a robe. "I'll get it," she yelled.

As she walked into the hall, she was still mulling over Bryony's earlier comment. Which kid would have heard she was the town "bad lady"?

The second least likely person she could think of was standing on her doorstep. While Maria stared, Leila pushed inside, clutching a crumpled piece of paper. "We have to talk. Someone's out to get you."

CHAPTER FIFTEEN

"WHAT ARE YOU TALKING ABOUT, Leila?"

"I wrote it all down." She stopped, taking in Maria's wet hair and robe. "Is my father here?"

Maria shook her head.

"Good. We have to call the police."

"What for?"

"Don't wait for the details. You need the cops. Now."

Leila's fear was too much after trying to reason with Jake and Bryony. The soft sofa and comforting, crackling fire, the spread of newspapers and homey disarray in her living room seemed to narrow into soft focus. "You are scaring me."

"I want you terrified. There's a kid in my day care class—"

"Your day care class?"

Leila held up both fists in frustration, and Maria shrugged. "Sorry. I don't understand how a kindergartner could threaten an adult."

"You know I work at the child care center a few mornings a week, before school. I'm not always assigned to the same room because of my classes at the college. Anyway, this kid is Griff's younger cousin, Billy."

"Oh. Don't worry. He's probably the one who told Bryony I was bad."

"Damn right he did. Where are you going?"

"To the kitchen. Do you want some coffee?"

Leila grabbed her with one hand and held out the paper ball with her other. "Forget the damn coffee and pay attention."

"I told you, Bryony already filled me in. Why am I the only one who finally believes the jury might be right?"

"Shut up and sit down."

Maria sat on the couch and waved Leila into a chair. "What else did the little boy say?"

"I wrote it down." Leila smoothed the sheet of paper over her knees as if she wanted to make sure she relayed every word. "He said his big cousin—that's Griff—was talking to Billy's mom about that picture in the paper."

"In the back of the paper," Maria said, because its location was its only saving grace and, surely, Leila would feel slightly better recalling that her father hadn't been on the front page. "Not that many fine citizens of

Honesty would have read past the Haney Furniture sale insert."

"Take me seriously," Leila said.

"You and I can't fix this. It's gossip. It doesn't matter. Time will fix it."

Leila shook her head. Her shiny hair swung around her shoulders and she looked younger than nineteen. "Billy said that Griff told his mother he should maybe stop you from saying he killed his parents."

Maria slid her hands down her thighs, drying her damp palms. "He said that in front of a smaller child? He had to be joking around."

"Billy was playing under the dining room table." Leila's dazed eyes frightened Maria more than the actual threats. "He said he was glad his mommy and Griff didn't know he was there because his mommy got really mad and said Griff had to stop doing that." She pressed the paper into Maria's chest. "That's exactly what Billy said. I wrote it down so I could tell the police, but I came to you first because you have to take yourself out of Griff's reach. He already got away with one murder."

Maria shook her head, turning Leila toward the hall. "I'm not going anywhere. Griff and his aunt were probably being sarcastic."

"Or not."

"Angela Hammond has told me several times that I'm the guilty one. If she could pin her sister and brother-in-law's murders on me, she'd find a way to do that, as well as blaming me for Griff's trial, but she doesn't believe for a second that Griff was guilty."

Leila veered out of Maria's reach. "I'm going to the cops. If you want to ignore a threat like this, fine, but you're not going to be on my conscience."

"Leila, don't." Maria held out her hand yet again, which Leila ignored. "Who, in this town, would believe you when you're trying to protect me?"

Their eyes met. Leila's earnest kindness touched Maria.

"I hate to say this," Maria said. "Maybe we should call your dad."

"My father?" Leila sank into the chair. "I don't understand."

"He's been trying to persuade Mr. and Mrs. Hammond to get help for Griff, and he's already talked to the police."

Leila knotted her fingers, unconvinced. "All right, but you should get your sister's evidence, too."

Maria raised her eyebrows.

"Yeah, I heard Billy tell Bryony he knew

she was your sister." She shrugged. "None of my business."

"Do you want to call your dad?" Maria rose and climbed over Leila's legs.

"I can't promise we won't argue."

"Same thing would happen if I called him."

She ran upstairs to Bryony's room and knocked on the door. Bryony didn't answer, so Maria called her name. She still didn't answer until Maria reached the bathroom.

"What are you doing?" Bryony poked her head around the shower curtain.

"Jake's daughter Leila's here. She talked to Billy."

"That's the kid who called you a bad lady."

"He said more than that. Rinse your hair. She's calling Jake, and he'll probably bring the police." She got a towel for Bryony and set it next to the shower. "Bryony, I'm glad you're here."

"Are you afraid?"

"Not necessarily of Griff."

JAKE GAVE UP trying to look detached. He leaned toward Tom, all his anger at Griff simmering closer to the surface than he would have liked. Tom had been his friend for years. "What do you mean you still can't touch him?"

"I said probably, Jake." The sheriff turned

toward Maria, who'd distanced herself from Jake upon his arrival and kept that distance since, as if they were performing some irritating dance whose steps he didn't understand. "Dr. Keaton," Tom said, "I can't promise we'll be able to do much with a note Leila wrote, based on the word of a four-year-old boy. We've found some evidence that might clear him of his parents' murders once and for all."

Bryony and Leila stared. Maria gasped, and Jake went to her. "It was that call I was waiting for. After my picture was in the paper, people started looking at my cases. I started looking." He hated admitting he might have been wrong in court. "There was a guy who assaulted his wife. He went to prison but then his brother threatened her about the time the Butlers died. The brother lived in Pennsylvania. We found a hunting accident involving a shotgun in his past. He got a parking ticket on the square the morning of the murder. His sister-in-law is staying with her brother, three houses down from the Butlers."

"Does that mean—" Maria was shaking. He wanted to hold her, but she'd never let him near him with all these people watching. Fortunately, Bryony edged closer to her sister.

"It means he's being investigated." Jake turned back to Tom. "But Griff still exhibits signs of being violent. I'm not suggesting an arrest, but let's intervene before he gets really angry. Maria has always felt he needed help."

Behind him, she exhaled and her relief was almost as good as an embrace. This time, he felt sure he was asking Tom to do the right thing.

"Even though I heard part of what his cousin said to Leila, too?" Bryony asked.

"He won't make the best witness."

"Tom," Jake began, "can't you talk to Griff and his aunt and uncle based on the threat? You need to know what he actually did the night his parents died if you want to go forward with the new suspect anyway."

"He may have made a possible threat. We don't know that the kid didn't misunderstand. I've called a friend of mine in child services. Because the kid overheard, he might be in danger if Griff is a bully, so he's our way into the house. I'll work on Griff through his relatives. They're not going to want to see their own child removed from the home."

"You can take a child, but you can't force Griff to get help?" Maria asked. Jake watched her worried expression. He'd missed her. He hated her being afraid, even for that thug kid and he felt guilty. His visit to the Hammonds might have made Griff angry all over again.

"I can threaten to take their child with a sympathetic child services officer as backup," Tom said. "If Griff doesn't crumble, that's all I can do."

"I'm—" Jake broke off. "I'd like to come with you."

Tom picked up his cap and nodded at Maria, Leila and Bryony before shaking his head at the judge. "Jake, old buddy, you've outlived your usefulness."

Even through a haze of frustration, Jake had to smile. "How long have you waited to say that?"

"Decades. Literally decades."

Tom nodded at Maria again, in the way of a small-town sheriff. "I'll probably drop back by to let you know what happens. Jake, you stay out of matters that don't concern you."

Maria walked him to the door, giving Jake a hilariously wide berth. Only Jake didn't feel like laughing, and he was even more irritated when he caught a glimpse of his daughter's amused smile. The two women in his life had adopted an "I told you so" smugness that was starting to piss him off.

By the time Maria returned, he'd prepared his argument against being thrown out. She stopped in front of him, eyeing him as if he were a stranger. "Thank you for trying to clear me. I'm glad about Griff," she said, and that was all.

"Let him stay," Bryony said behind her. "He's been worried about you, and Leila's in this now, too."

Maria's rigid stance wavered. She glanced toward Leila, then back at her sister.

"Clowns," she said, and left the room.

"Where's she going?" Jake asked.

Within seconds, a crash from the kitchen answered his question.

"We needed to wash some dishes," Bryony said with a quick grin at Leila. "I guess breaking them all is another way to empty the sink. I'll see if I can help her."

"Bryony, we're only investigating the other guy. His visit to town might be a coincidence. Maria still needs to be wary of Griff."

Bryony nodded.

After she left, Jake risked one more rejection, moving to his daughter's side on the couch. "You okay?" he asked.

"Yeah. I don't know why you had to talk to the Hammonds."

"I'm not surprised you think I was wrong."

"You know what, Dad? An acquittal didn't help that kid. He needs another therapist, or an anger management program, or something to smooth the rough edges of his out-of-body experiences. For once, I'd have thought telling his aunt and uncle what you discovered was right, except your visit to their house made him angrier, and he's frightened Maria."

"She doesn't seem to have your common sense, honey. She's not afraid."

"She should be when she stops being mad at you." Leila put her hand on his shoulder and gave him a little shove. "Go see her."

"You don't mind?"

"She's my friend, too, and I don't want to lose her because you're a jerk."

"Am I, Leila?"

"Kind of," she said. "But don't let that weigh on your conscience. You never have before."

"I do feel bad about the past," he said. "That's why I've been trying to see you since I found out Maria was your psychologist."

"I don't want to talk about it."

"I've run a courtroom for nearly ten years, but I can't find an appeal that reaches two stubborn women."

"That is correct."

"I didn't expect to feel this uncertain at my age."

"MARIA?"

She nearly dropped the plate she was handing to Bryony when Jake spoke from the kitchen door. Bryony, ever subtle, set plate and tea towel on the counter and bounded for the hall.

"Thanks," Jake said as she neared him. She nodded, muttered something unintelligible and stepped on his feet on her way past.

Maria laughed at his flinch. "Imagine if she was wearing her big work shoes," she said.

"I don't want to share clown jokes." He crossed the room and touched a dollop of soap bubbles locked into a wave of her hair. She pulled back.

"You don't know what it means to me that you've tried to clear my name. I thought having you believe in me would make everything right. But then you made it all worse. Maybe you can't see that interfering—"

"I see."

"Oh. That lets the air out of me." She turned back to the sink. He picked up Bryony's tea towel. She eyed it, her hands deep in soapy water. "What if I asked you to go back out there?"

"I'd go. Leila's having such a good time snubbing me."

"I don't feel bad for you," Maria said, but the hours since she'd left his house had doused the angry flame in her green eyes.

She was soft again, and he wanted to hold her. He wanted to hold her every time he was near enough to wrap his arms around her subtle curves.

"You have empathy, though," he said. "You've been an outcast. You know how lonely I am without you and Leila."

She ignored his opening. "I'm surprised you didn't force your way into Sheriff Drake's car."

"Angela Hammond is about one confrontation away from shooting you and me down on the courthouse square, and they won't persuade Griff to consider explaining what happened at his parents' home, if his aunt is banging around him in a rage."

"They probably won't get him to talk. She's reinforced his anger. Her support has probably convinced him he's been right all along." Without thinking, she rinsed a plate and passed it on. "You should talk to Leila."

"She won't talk, but she is bending. She sent me in here."

"She was afraid when she came to warn me about Griff. She needs you."

"I need both of you."

With a soapy hand, Maria plucked the towel from him. "That's not going to happen."

He held on to the towel's hem as if it were a connection that bound them. "Don't avoid the subject of us. What kind of psychologist pretends nothing is happening when something most definitely is? Are you afraid to get involved with me? Because I'm not afraid, Maria."

"I don't care if this means I'm bad at my job." She tugged until he wasn't holding the terry cloth anymore. "I want to be good at life, too. I want to believe in you and trust that you won't override what I'm thinking and feeling, that you won't run with what's best in your mind, instead of what matters most to me."

"So we live a relationship your way or no way at all?" He started for the door. "I've had experience with that approach."

"No. You can't dismiss me with some barb about your past. The problem is, when you decide what you think is best, considering what I want doesn't even occur to you."

He stood at the door, suddenly tired of being completely at fault. "We jumped into a relationship before we knew anything about each other. I had a picture of you in my mind, and I thought it was you."

"I still think you are the picture you gave me."

Jake didn't know what to say. He gave up. "I'm not asking you to be someone else," he finally said. "I'll wait in the other room. Tom and the others should be back soon, no matter what happens at the Hammonds."

But then he couldn't walk away. He went to

her, sliding his arms around her, bending though she had to stand on tiptoes as he looked into her eyes. "I thought you'd fight for what you want," he said. "I'd fight for you."

"I've tried. But deep down neither of us understands what the other needs."

He kissed her again until they were both breathing hard, both too deep in their need for each other to be sensible. So he thought.

"I don't care about Griff Butler. I don't care what comes next. When you touch me I want you, and yet I can't let myself be a woman who lets a man obliterate everything else that matters to her."

His heart broke a little. Wasn't she talking about how love felt?

"I won't promise everything will be okay," he said. And after a few seconds, he left.

"DAD, I HATE TO SEE you like this." Leila dropped onto the couch beside him, and the whole floor seemed to echo with her thud. He smiled, grateful because she helped ease his sense of emptiness.

"I'm all right," he said.

"You're such a liar." She leaned against his shoulder. "And I'm getting sleepy. I have early class in the morning."

"Do you need to study?"

"Don't break the mood, okay?"

Within a few minutes, her head drooped onto his shoulder again, and then her breathing grew even.

He tried to release his arm to put it around her, but her sleepy complaint kept him where he was.

It wasn't that hard to let well enough alone.

Time must have passed. Bryony never showed up again. Maria stayed busy in the kitchen. The familiar sounds of dishes and silver clattering should have been comforting. Instead, every move Maria made in there was a pointed reminder that he wouldn't be here again. He couldn't depend on Griff Butler and Angela Hammond to pry open a door at Maria's for him every evening.

Finally, the doorbell rang. Jake eased away from Leila. He reached the hall to find Maria and Bryony halfway down the stairs. He put out his hand.

"Stay there."

Oddly, they did. He leaned to the right for a glimpse of the crowd on Maria's porch. Griff Butler waited in front of Tom, as if Tom were holding him between fatherly hands. Jake sought Maria's gaze.

"It's Griff."

"What?" She came down.

"Bryony, get Leila and take her upstairs," Jake said.

"Okay." She hurried into the living room. Jake maintained his spot by the door, between that kid and the women. Tom rang the bell again. Leila appeared in the hall.

"Dad, he's here? Did his aunt come, too?"

"Please go with Bryony," he said, tucking his hand beneath her chin. "I'm sure it'll be fine, but I really don't want Griff seeing you."

"Maria, come with us," she said.

Maria shook her head. "I have to face him. We have to stop the threats and anger, or he'll never get healthy."

Jake finally understood her frustration with his inability to veer from his sense of duty. He wished he had the right to insist she go with her sister and his daughter. Again, the bell rang. Jake ignored it until Bryony and Leila were out of sight.

When he opened the door, Tom looked as if he might like to make arrests all around. "Where were you?"

"Here," Jake said. "Griff, what are you doing here?"

"We need to talk," Tom said. "Griff has some things he wants to tell Dr. Keaton."

Maria came to Jake's side. He barely managed

to keep from stepping in front of her. Griff didn't cut an intimidating figure, but he'd hurt Maria in long-lasting ways already.

"Come in," she said. "Can I get anyone a coffee? Anything?"

"No," Jake said, unable to stop himself.

Tom looked amused as he urged Griff inside and nodded some unspoken command to the patrol officers behind them.

In the living room, Jake sat beside Maria. He took her hand with the intent of leaving Griff in no doubt about whom he'd face if he threatened her again.

Maria didn't even notice. "Are you all right?" she asked the kid. "Have you been seeing someone else?" She glanced at Tom. "A therapist, I mean?"

"Why do you care?" Griff asked.

"Because you and I know what happened between us. I always wanted you to be well, and that's all I wanted."

"I told him the truth," Griff said, jutting a shoulder toward the sheriff.

"And now he wants to explain to you so that we can end all the drama in this town," Tom said. "It's time everyone got back to a normal life, and I find the person or people who killed this boy's family."

"I'm not a boy," Griff said, apparently missing the important points of Tom's speech.

Maria did not. "I never believed you did it," she said. "That's why I gave you time to take it back."

"I loved you," the boy said in a broken voice that almost appealed to Jake's sympathy. Crazy or not, kid or not, it hurt a guy to love a woman who didn't love him in return.

"You didn't," Maria said. "You mistook gratitude for something more intense. But what happened to your parents?"

"I don't know. I found them—" he stopped for a jaw-clenching moment, while his eyes grew red and he breathed too hard "—like I told the sheriff all along. But you were nicer to me afterward, and I thought you might be falling for me, too. When you told me to stop talking about the way I felt, I thought I had to get your attention again. So I made up that story. I thought you couldn't tell anyone what I said at your office."

"Even after I warned you I had to tell the police?"

"I didn't think you would. You liked me."

"I cared about you the same way I cared about all my clients. Maybe I felt sorry for you because of your parents, but I told you I had to report crimes."

"I couldn't let you think I was a liar."

"Griff." She covered her face with her hands. "Your parents' murderer may be long gone."

"I know," he said, a sob shaking his shoulders so that even Jake wanted to give the boy a comforting pat. Which hadn't happened that often in his years on the bench. "But Sheriff Drake said they're looking for another guy."

"You got in so much trouble," Maria said. "I may lose my job. Even Judge Sloane is in trouble around here because you and your aunt have lied about us both."

"Aunt Angela is so angry with me she won't have time to talk to anyone else about anything for a couple of months."

Maria cracked a hint of a smile. Jake wanted to yank her close. The kid might be harmless, but he saw no reason for her to get near Griff again.

"Are you seeing another therapist?"

"I have the names you sent my aunt."

Jake turned his head. Maria had no right to talk about foolish interference.

"Call those guys and see if one of them can help you." She offered her hand to Tom. "Thanks. I needed this."

He nodded. "You both did. We're going on to the station to take a statement and continue working on the Butlers' case. Jake, I'd like to get those files back."

Jake nodded. "I'll drop them off in the morning."

"Good enough." Tom directed Griff back toward the hall. "Night, folks."

"Good night," Maria said. At least she made no offer of solace to the boy.

They walked to the door. After Tom and Griff left with uncomfortable nods and more abrupt good-nights, Maria caught the doorknob.

"Why don't you go up and get Leila? Unless she's asleep in a guest room, you should walk her to her door."

"You won't talk to me, Maria?"

She barely looked at him. "I told you, I thought this was the most important thing between us, but we still look at the world differently. Nothing's changed."

"I don't see it that way. That trial has finally ended. You're bound to get your license back after the board hears about Griff's confession."

She narrowed her gaze. "Don't even think of approaching that board, Jake."

He turned away. His first thought had been hope that she'd get her career back, and that maybe they'd work out a way to be together when life returned to normal. Her first thought had been horror that he'd try to help her.

CHAPTER SIXTEEN

MARIA WENT BACK to her odd jobs, but they couldn't keep her from thinking about Jake. She loved him. She loved him not.

Who was she kidding? She loved him. When her resolve to stay away threatened to weaken, she repeated all her reasons for refusing to see him.

Each night, in long hours of loneliness, she dialed Jake's number more than once. If she wasn't careful, she'd hit the button that connected the call.

"Do you like living in limbo?"

Startled by Bryony's voice, Maria jabbed the lamp she'd been dusting, but caught it just before it landed on the floor. "I thought you had a party this afternoon."

"Nope. What's the deal with you and Jake? Are you trying to salvage your pride? Can you be this upset because a man loves you?"

"You saw him. He marched in here and started ordering us around."

"Because his daughter was here. They don't know for sure the other guy is guilty. If you and the sheriff had been wrong about Griff, Leila might have been in danger. Maybe you really regret sleeping with Jake before you got a contract that spelled out the terms of your mutual commitment."

A quick ambush by sensual memories made her sit down. "There's nothing wrong with wanting to be safe."

"Jake would agree with you. He'd go one further. He wanted you to be safe, and he wanted his daughter to be safe, too. That's why he interfered."

"You're on his side because you and Mom don't mind if some guy shows up with all the answers. You want a man to step in and run your lives. I don't. I need one who respects my feelings even more when he doesn't agree with them. I don't want to disappear inside someone else's decisions." The moment she finished speaking, she dropped her dusting cloth, horrified at her outburst.

"That's not fair, Maria. I'm not like that now. I'm not even sure Mom is."

Maria wiped her hands on her jeans. "You're absolutely right. I'm sorry. I'm frightened because I keep trying to find reasons to give in."

"I am living proof that people can change."

"Lasting change is rare, and I'm not sure Jake sees a problem with managing my life."

"I don't know." Bryony pounded a sofa cushion into submission. "I can remember… Anyway, you usually take me at my word."

"You won't break my heart."

"Don't fool yourself. Sisters can do that."

"I'm so ashamed of all the disapproving I did, Bryony."

"Well, when we do break each other's hearts, what do we do?"

"We talk. We work it out."

"I don't know how you feel about taking advice from a clown, but do you love Jake less than you love me? You're both private people, and maybe you're stinging from all the publicity. He's made himself a spectacle, trying to help you. You love each other enough to change. You both already have."

Outside, the letter box by the door clattered. Maria put down her polish and opened the front door. The mail carrier, already on his way next door, waved. Maria waved back and yanked her mail out of the box.

She came back inside, shivering. "It's freezing. I think we're up for more snow."

"Bottom line, Maria, you won't have to become someone like Mom to live with Jake."

Maria hated that being her worst fear. "How do you know?"

"I know you, and if you think this over, instead of being afraid, you'll realize you know him, and nothing will be perfect, but being with him will be worth making it work."

"That sounds good," Maria said, turning over her letters. She clenched one from the Psychology Review Board. "Bryony?"

"Huh?"

"This is it."

"The letter? Don't freak. You're going to be fine. They— Open it."

She did, tearing the envelope diagonally. The single page trembled between her fingers. "'Dear, Dr. Kea… We apologize… Sheriff Tom Drake appeared before us with an affidavit, as well as bringing one from the young man in question, whom you'll be relieved to know is seeing a qualified therapist. We welcome you back to the prof…'" She crumpled the letter. "I'm free."

"Like hell," Bryony said as she laughed with joy. "You know you'll still be walking those demon dogs."

"Let's go find champagne." Maria started up

the stairs, her sister hot on her heels. "Did you notice? Only Sheriff Drake appeared before them. I half assumed Jake would find a reason to go, too."

"That's what I've been saying. Maybe it's your turn to make a change."

ON CHRISTMAS EVE, Leila brought her things to stay over at Jake's. Together, they made dinner and avoided the subject of Maria until they were trimming the tree, when Leila finally exploded.

"You're not the same man you were, Dad. Don't settle like you did with Mom. Go tell Maria exactly what you want."

"I want her to trust me." He needed her to need him. How did a man say that to a woman who'd asked him to stay away from her? She either loved him or she didn't, and the past week had assured him she didn't.

"I know what it's like when you assume other people are coping better than they actually are. Naturally, she's annoyed."

"Naturally." He passed his daughter a big, red ornament. "I'm going to do you a favor, because there's a little of me in you. Never assume someone you love will forgive you after you make a decision for him."

"You meant no harm."

"She wants me to discuss the important things with her, and I tried, but she kept shutting me down. I was right, you know."

"You were, this time." Leila hung the ornament, backed up and then moved it to a different spot. "But, Dad, you were never right about protecting me. I'd have understood Mom had a problem."

"I'm sorry," he said. "But I never knew how to explain, and I didn't want you to think badly of your mother."

"I'm saying give a woman room. If she loves you, she won't be able to give up. I didn't give up on you, Dad."

He looked at her.

"I love you enough to keep coming back when you backslide. Talk to Maria. She helped me understand second chances."

"You have to get along with me. You're my daughter."

"I had to trust you'd finally talk about what really happened and be honest with me—that we'd share the problems in our family, rather than you wrapping them up, all fixed in a nice bow. If I hadn't trusted you, daughter or not, I'd have given up on you when I lost Maria." Leila rolled up her sleeves to show off fading scars. "Notice I've changed, too. Maria may be afraid you can't harness the Machiavelli in you, but she's in the business of change."

MARIA MADE Bryony Christmas breakfast and carried it up to her room. She plumped up the stocking that included a gift card for a bookstore, and a few small things.

There was no answer at her sister's bedroom door. "Bryony?"

She knocked again. Still, no answer. Maria balanced the tray on one arm and opened the bedroom door. It was empty. The comforter trailed onto the floor. Clothes littered a path past her feet, toward the shower, but the bathroom was empty.

"Hmm."

Nothing to do but take her sister's tray back to the kitchen. She poured herself a cup of coffee before she dug into eggs and bacon.

The front door banged open. Wind and sleigh bell sounds rushed through the small house.

"Santa?" she asked with a smile. This was Christmas day, after all. "Bryony, where'd you take the reindeer?"

"To pick me up."

Leaning to see into the hall, Maria nearly fell out of her chair. "Mom?"

Gail Keaton seemed uncertain of her welcome. Maria ran to her mother, who backed up under the onslaught. Maria grabbed her and held on. Tears prickled beneath her eyelids.

"I'm so glad you're here," she said.

"It is Christmas. I came to see if you bought me any more presents."

"You did not." Maria held out her arms to Bryony behind their mother and all three hugged. It was like coming home. At last. Home to her mother and her sister. Home to herself.

"I love you," she said to them.

"She's a little emotional these days." Bryony patted Maria's head.

"Don't you make fun of her. She's always afraid we'll do something crazy. It's a big day when she can say she loves me without sounding just a little scared."

"I'm not making fun." Bryony nudged the door shut with her foot. "Let's see what we got each other."

First, Maria scrambled more eggs and cooked extra bacon. They ate quickly, all grabbing a second cup of coffee before they settled in front of the tree in the living room. Gail had stopped on the way to fish bright packages out of her bags. She set them in her daughters' laps.

"Mom, did you unwrap the things we sent you already?" Bryony asked.

"Yes, but I'm anxious to see what you think of yours."

Bryony and Maria tore into their presents the way they had as children. Maria buried her nose in the soft pink scarf and cloche cap her mother had knitted. "When did you learn to do this?"

"I'm taking a hiatus from dating." She nudged Bryony, who was holding a similar pile of pale green. "But a girl's gotta do something with her hands."

For once, all three laughed together. Then the doorbell rang.

Maria's heart did a quick rumba in her chest. She couldn't speak. Jake might have stayed away from the review board, but had he been able to stay away from her?

"Go answer it," Bryony said.

"What am I missing?" Gail asked.

"I hope you're missing Mr.-Just-Perfect-for-Maria. You'll like him, but we must stay here because they haven't been playing well together." Her warning gaze was Maria's anchor. "Coming here today took courage," Bryony said.

"Doesn't he have family of his own?"

"A daughter, Mom. Let Maria see if it's him."

Maria climbed around her mother and sister. Bryony's low voice murmured as Maria headed toward the door with the grace of a woman trudging through quicksand.

"It took courage," Bryony said again.

Maria turned back.

Her sister bit her lip, but then sped on to get out everything she had to say fast. "Don't hide behind a mask of respect and responsibility. Love the man. Isn't your happiness disappearing because you're so determined to live without him?"

Bryony saw pretty clearly for a girl who made her living behind a mask.

Maria opened the door, almost sick. What if it wasn't him?

But she knew. Before she touched that doorknob, she knew.

"Merry Christmas," he said, and he looked like himself—confident, gorgeous, with a hint of unease in his dark gaze.

So she hadn't forced him to become a man he couldn't be. "Come in Jake. Come out of the cold."

Silence stretched between them. All she could think was that he'd returned. He'd had more courage than she. He'd kept trying.

He watched her as she took his hand and pulled him inside. "How do you mean that?"

"The cold of not being together," she said, "where I think we might belong."

"What suddenly makes you think that?" he asked.

Her happiness took a dive. "You don't?"

"It's what I came to tell you." His gaze caressed her. She was lucky.

"I have to stop being stubborn," she said. "And afraid."

"What scared you so much?"

"I don't want to lose myself because I love you."

"You—" He kissed her swiftly. "Do you love me?"

"I can't help myself."

"But why aren't you happy, Maria? Loving you makes me happy."

"First you didn't believe me. Then you interfered every time I asked you not to. I even think you browbeat Helen's friends into giving me work."

His skin took on a heated flush, despite the winter air.

"You did," she said.

"I'd let you starve now," he said, kindness and husky affection belying his words.

"You didn't go to the board. And yet you didn't give up on me. You came here. And you're not too angry to forgive me for holding out."

"I'm not an idiot." He twined their fingers.

His were as cold as ice, and she didn't care. He was all the heat she wanted. "But I should have gone to that board."

Maria grinned. She tiptoed to kiss his cheek. "You're more than a man of steel. Do you think you can deny yourself again if I have to make my own decisions?"

"You ask the impossible," he said with an exaggerated sigh. "We both have a say in what's right for us. I want it that way, too."

He kissed her, his hands desperate as he stroked her back and her waist. Maria almost cried. It was so good to hold him again, to feel his muscles flexing against her palms, and the heat of his breath in her mouth. As he slid his hands beneath her breasts, he lifted his head. "Can we talk about marriage sometime soon?"

Her feet didn't seem to work, and neither did her legs. She felt as if she were hovering above herself.

"I know," he said, his mouth against her temple. "We hardly know each other. You think I'm a bully because I want to run my loved ones' lives."

"You say you aren't afraid, but I think something scares you into taking control that doesn't belong to you."

"Losing," he said. "I want control so I can make sure I won't lose anyone who matters to me."

"Control makes me want to run."

"So I'm learning to let it go," he said. "Slowly. For instance, I'm not asking you to marry me today. Take your time. Make certain. I'm just telling you now because all the time in the world, all the days that pass, won't make me more certain. I love you. When you're ready— if you're ready—you tell me."

She breathed again. "I always insist feelings matter most, but I've been giving in to the wrong kind."

He kissed her forehead, hugging her so close she could hardly speak. She couldn't— wouldn't—move away from him. "I'll never break a promise to you again, Maria."

"Jake," she said, slipping to her knees. She expected him to follow, but he stood over her, bewildered. "I can ask you from down here," she said, "but it'll be more fun if you join me."

He knelt in slow motion. "Are you sure?" he asked.

"And terrified. I could live without you," she said. "But I'd feel empty every day without you in it."

"You don't need time to consider?"

"I love you. Love isn't always safe with you, or wise." She smiled against his cheek. "But it's real between us, and I'm grabbing it." She took his face between her hands. With her lips barely over his, she asked, "Will you marry me?"

He kissed her, claiming her, offering and taking with his mouth and his hands, and making his answer clear.

"I need to hear you say yes," she said, leaning back.

"Yes." He took her mouth again, and she forgot her mother and sister and the hard floor beneath her knees.

"Wait." He slid his hands over her with restless hunger. "We have to tell Leila."

"Will she see you?"

"She stayed at my house last night. She browbeat me into coming here."

"Let's go tell her together. I think she and my sister may be the smarter therapists. Maybe we can start a family practice." She grabbed her coat and gloves from the hall closet. "Can we tell Mom and Bryony first?"

"Mom?" Jake said. "Your mother's here? Are you all right?"

"You said something, dear?"

Maria turned just in time to see her mother inspect Jake with her best up-and-down, "what a big boy you are" glance. Clearly, knitting wasn't doing its job.

Again, the doorbell rang. Maria answered it

instead of lecturing her mother on inappropriate come-ons. Gail usually accused her of
being envious because she hadn't mastered the
art of flirting.

Leila, hopping from one booted foot to the
other, hurried inside. "I couldn't wait." She stared
from her father to Maria. "You look happy."

Maria hugged her, as tight as she could, and
then turned her around. "Leila, you'd better
meet my mother. You'll be family when your
dad and I decide on the right month and day."

"Will we?"

The celebratory group hug was more like a
football scrum, and no one came out untouched.
Gail finally staggered to freedom, tidying her hair.

"We need wine," she said. "I don't suppose
my own dear temperance-minded daughter has
a bottle stashed for the holidays?"

"Funny, Mom. Bryony and I drank the tiny
bottle we could afford last night."

"I have champagne," Jake said. "Come with
me to get it, Maria."

"Leila?" Maria said.

"I'll stay here and get to know your mother."
They turned as one toward the kitchen. "What are
you all cooking? Dad didn't even buy a turkey."

"Just champagne?" Gail asked. "I like that
guy."

"There must have been a sale," Leila said. "My dad's kind of cheap."

Maria laughed until Jake stopped her with a kiss. He slid his hands inside her coat. Before long, she wanted to throw it aside.

"No." He pulled his hands away and urged her toward the door.

She wreaked her revenge as he drove. A chaste kiss on the corner of his mouth turned into insistence that led her fingers to the buttons on his shirt and down to his waistband.

Fortunately, he owned one of the few houses in his neighborhood with an attached garage. A trail of clothes followed them into his kitchen.

The coldness of the granite counter made Maria hiss in shock. Pausing only to undo her bra, Jake slid his palm between her and the stone.

"Come upstairs," he said, lowering his mouth to her breast. "No more floors."

"This isn't a floor. It's a counter." She arched into him, begging for now instead of upstairs.

He sighed, holding her head, only to echo her gasp as she found his taut nipple.

"They won't expect us back for a while," he said, catching her in his arms.

She wrapped her legs around his waist. "I still don't need a bed."

"For everything I want to do to you, a bed will be more comfortable."

He was a strong man. He carried her up a set of back stairs, to a small room where they saw Christmas morning in with love almost too perfect to believe.

At last they sprawled, Maria on her stomach, Jake lying half across her back, with one leg between hers.

"What will next Christmas bring?" Maria asked.

Jake pushed her hair across her face, and kissed the pulse beating at the side of her throat. "All I need to know is that I'll wake up with you."

EPILOGUE

A TINY FIST WAVED in the air, welcoming the next Christmas morning with the sweetest of all greetings. Maria's infant daughter snuffled a little. "You're fine." Maria nuzzled her baby's nose, wondering if she'd ever look at her without awe. "Daddy's paying the bill, and then we'll go home and lock the world out and just be us together."

Her hospital door burst open, and Leila followed it into her room.

"Where's your dad?" Maria asked, making room for one more on the bed.

"With your mother. She's—"

"Doing one of her slow strolls, gathering an audience," Bryony said, coming into the room but going straight to the baby. "Isn't she beautiful? What did you name her?"

"Maria, I wouldn't leave Dad alone with your mother too often." Leila pitched her voice low.

"Don't take this personally, but I think Gail's putting the moves on him."

"There's a question that's been on my mind for some time," Gail said, sweeping into the room, her hand wrapped like a python around Jake's forearm. Maybe like a cobra. He couldn't seem to look away.

"What's the question, Mom?" Bryony asked.

"Just get it over with," Maria said, grinning, as she held out her daughter to Leila.

"Are there any more at home like you?" Gail asked Jake.

Maria and Leila and Bryony burst into laughter that startled their sleepy baby. Jake extricated himself from Gail's clutches as she looked stunned at their mockery.

"What did you name our girl?" Bryony asked again.

"Bryony Leila Gail," Jake said, standing close enough for Maria to touch him.

Leila turned. Gail grabbed for the bed rail. Bryony burst into tears.

"Now, B." Jake hugged his sister-in-law, cradling her head on his shoulder.

Maria touched Leila's cheek. She couldn't read the younger woman's wide stare. "You don't mind that she shares your name? We haven't signed anything yet."

"Mind?" Her whisper broke. "She's my family, my baby sister." Leila leaned her head against Maria's. "And I'm proud."

"You named her after me, too?" Gail sat on the bed. "You named her after me, Maria."

"I had a hand in it." Jake held one daughter while leaning down to nuzzle the other.

"Yeah, but you don't know me," Gail said.

"I'd do anything to please your daughter." He kissed his wife. "I trust her judgment."

"He had the names on the form before I knew we'd agreed. I wanted Christmas." Maria grinned as every eyebrow in the room cocked. "Carol."

"Uh-huh." Leila ignored her completely to nudge her father in the ribs. "I knew you couldn't change. You still know best."

"You're wrong." His eyes promised Maria everything. Everything she'd ever dreamed of, and all she hoped for in the future. "And it's lucky for your sister that Maria trusts me, or little Bryony would be stuck with a hokey name."

"I knew I could trust him after he agreed to my new home office," Maria said.

Leila nodded sagely. "I don't know how many times he told my mom and me that work stayed in the office downtown." She turned to her father. "You're balancing work and home right now, Dad."

Maria reached for Jake because Leila's observation seemed to pinch a little.

"I didn't mean to complain, and I'm over the mommy-and-daddy-back-together fixation. You weren't right for each other," Leila said quickly.

"But am I doing right by you and all these other women, Leila?" Jake asked, and she hugged him, laughing. Father and daughter laughed together a lot these days.

There was no better music to Maria's ears.

"I have to ask again." Gail eased daintily into Maria's waiting wheelchair, giving Jake all her attention, ignoring the orderly trying to shoo her out. "Are there any more at home like you?"

"Mom, leave him alone." Maria stood. Everyone came at her, but then Jake handed little Bry back to Leila and wrapped his arm around Maria. She looped her arm around his waist, perfectly well, but content to start the future in her husband's embrace. "This family belongs to all of us." She grinned, blissful. "But this man? He's all mine."

* * * * *

*Celebrate 60 years of pure reading
pleasure with Harlequin®!
Just in time for the holidays,
Silhouette Special Edition® is proud to present
New York Times bestselling author
Kathleen Eagle's
ONE COWBOY, ONE CHRISTMAS*

Rodeo rider Zach Beaudry was a travelin'
man—until he broke down in middle-of-
nowhere South Dakota during a deep freeze.
That's when an angel came to his rescue....

"Don't die on me. Come on, Zel. You know how much I love you, girl. You're all I've got. Don't do this to me here. Not *now*."

But Zelda had quit on him, and Zach Beaudry had no one to blame but himself. He'd taken his sweet time hitting the road, and then miscalculated a shortcut. For all he knew he was a hundred miles from gas. But even if they were sitting next to a pump, the ten dollars he had in his pocket wouldn't get him out of South Dakota, which was not where he wanted to be right now. Not even his beloved pickup truck, Zelda, could get him much of anywhere on fumes. He was sitting out in the cold in the middle of nowhere. And getting colder.

He shifted the pickup into Neutral and pulled hard on the steering wheel, using the downhill slope to get her off the blacktop and into the roadside grass, where she shuddered to a standstill. He stroked the padded dash. "You'll be safe here."

But Zach would not. It was getting dark, and it was already too damn cold for his cowboy ass. Zach's battered body was a barometer, and he was feeling South Dakota, big time. He'd have given his right arm to be climbing into a hotel hot tub instead of a brutal blast of north wind. The right was his free arm anyway. Damn thing had lost altitude, touched some part of the bull and caused him a scoreless ride last time out.

It wasn't scoring him a ride this night, either. A carload of teenagers whizzed by, topping off the insult by laying on the horn as they passed him. It was at least twenty minutes before another vehicle came along. He stepped out and waved both arms this time, damn near getting himself killed. Whatever happened to *do unto others?* In places like this, decent people didn't leave each other stranded in the cold.

His face was feeling stiff, and he figured he'd better start walking before his toes went numb.

He struck out for a distant yard light, the only sign of human habitation in sight. He couldn't tell how distant, but he knew he'd be hurting by the time he got there, and he was counting on some kindly old man to be answering the door. No shame among the lame.

It wasn't like Zach was fresh off the operating table—it had been a few months since his last round of repairs—but he hadn't given himself enough time. He'd lopped a couple of weeks off the near end of the doc's estimated recovery time, rigged up a brace, done some heavy-duty taping and climbed onto another bull. Hung in there for five seconds—four seconds past feeling the pop in his hip and three seconds short of the buzzer.

He could still feel the pain shooting down his leg with every step. Only this time he had to pick the damn thing up, swing it forward and drop it down again on his own.

Pride be damned, he just hoped *somebody* would be answering the door at the end of the road. The light in the front window was a good sign.

The four steps to the covered porch might as well have been four hundred, and he was looking to climb them with a lead weight chained to his left leg. His eyes were just as screwed up as his hip. Big black spots danced around with tiny red flashers, and he couldn't tell what was real and what wasn't. He stumbled over some shrubbery, steadied himself on the porch railing and peered between vertical slats.

There in the front window stood a spruce tree with a silver star affixed to the top. Zach was pretty sure the red sparks were all in his head, but the white lights twinkling by the hundreds throughout the huge tree, those were real. He wasn't too sure about the woman hanging the shiny balls. Most of her hair was caught up on her head and fastened in a curly clump, but the light captured by the escaped bits crowned her with a golden halo. Her face was a soft shadow, her body a willowy silhouette beneath a long white gown. If this was where the mind ran off to when cold started shutting down the rest of the body, then Zach's final worldly thought was, *This ain't such a bad way to go.*

If she would just turn to the window, he could die looking into the eyes of a Christmas angel.

* * * * *

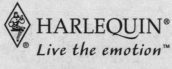

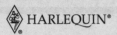

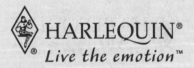

HARLEQUIN®
INTRIGUE®

BREATHTAKING ROMANTIC SUSPENSE

Shared dangers and passions lead to electrifying
romance and heart-stopping suspense!

Every month, you'll meet six new heroes
who are guaranteed to make your spine tingle
and your pulse pound. With them you'll enter
into the exciting world of Harlequin Intrigue—
where your life is on the line
and so is your heart!

THAT'S INTRIGUE—
ROMANTIC SUSPENSE
AT ITS BEST!

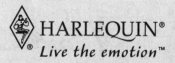

HARLEQUIN®
Live the emotion™

www.eHarlequin.com   INTDIR06

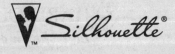

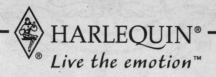

Harlequin® Historical
Historical Romantic Adventure!

Imagine a time of chivalrous knights and unconventional ladies, roguish rakes and impetuous heiresses, rugged cowboys and spirited frontierswomen— these rich and vivid tales will capture your imagination!

Harlequin Historical . . . they're too good to miss!